YASMIN MEETS A YAK

By
OLIVE L. GROOM

LONDON
PICKERING & INGLIS LTD.
1972

PICKERING & INGLIS LTD.
29 LUDGATE HILL, LONDON, EC4M 7JQ
26 BOTHWELL STREET, GLASGOW, G2 6PA

ISBN 0 7208 2194 0
Cat. No. 11/1602

Printed in Great Britain by Northumberland Press Limited, Gateshead

CONTENTS

The Birthday

1

"IT'S MEAN, MEAN! HE KNOWS IT'S MY BIRTH-day," wailed Gerda, halfway between anger and tears of disappointment. "He promised."

"Don't speak like that about Dad." Yasmin spoke sharply for once. "You know a doctor can't just walk off and leave his patients the minute it's tea-time. Be your age, do!"

Gerda looked sulky, her pretty oval face flushed. Although she was only a year younger than her sister she had always been treated as the family baby and was a little spoilt as a result.

"Well, he did promise to be home early," she muttered resentfully. "It's always the same whenever it's something for us. Everyone else yells for what they want and Dad goes running at once. It's only his own family who have to wait and take a back seat. Well, I'm tired of it—and of this rotten place and—and everything."

This time temper and tears took over and Gerda dashed from the room, crying stormily. Yasmin sighed sharply as echoes of the door slamming died away. Then she went on mechanically arranging plates of cake and fruit on the tea table, her expression serious. The trouble was that there was a certain amount of genuine foundation for Gerda's complaints: their father, Dr. Oake, as the only medical practitioner in this remote district of India was always overworked and his daughters were forced to take second place under the constant pressure. There was always so much suffering and so many calls upon Dr. Oake's time that he was seldom able to spend more than a few moments each day with his family. They understood because it had always been so for as long as they could remember, and usually they tried to be patient and uncomplaining. Occasionally, however, Gerda at least found the situation too hard to bear, hence today's outburst.

"It was different when Mum was alive," Yasmin thought unhappily and then shrugged slightly. She could not honestly say that she remembered much about their mother, not enough to feel sad about her, anyway. Mrs. Oake had died when Gerda was just five and Yasmin six, so that both girls had only a vague memory of her. Their creature comforts had been looked after by a succession of ayahs, Indian nursemaids, kindly and gentle, and in general they had been happy enough until recently. Together with other girls of their age in Leolali they went by bus each day to the High School some miles away in the only town of any size and shared a European-style education. They had not noticed their uniqueness in being the only non-Indian girls in the school until last term, but once they had done so Gerda had become restless and impatient.

"If only those girls from the Embassy hadn't come last term we would have been O.K.," Yasmin thought now ruefully, finishing laying the table and going over to sit on the verandah rail, staring unseeingly at the familiar dusty, rutted road and the small huddle of houses that was Leolali. "It was hearing them talk of England and—and home things that made Gerda unsettled. Not that she can remember much about it, any more than I can—except Grannie's big house and the dogs and playing with the

6

snow once. I suppose we are rather isolated here and no one could call Leolali a beautiful place. It wouldn't be so bad, though, if Dad were at home more. Anyway, the Embassy girls are going back home next week so perhaps Gerda will settle down again soon."

The younger girl had certainly calmed down when she came back to eat her birthday tea some thirty minutes later; nevertheless there was an obstinate set to her mouth and determined chin that made Yasmin uneasy. In the absence of their father she usually bore the brunt of the younger girl's tantrums and, being a peaceful soul herself, she shrank from high-powered arguments and temper displays.

"I'm all for a quiet life," she would often say, and so put off unpleasant decisions or the facing of uncomfortable facts rather more than was good for her. It was Gerda who always made the fuss and outcry over anything; Yasmin preferred to ignore what she did not like and only wanted to jog along in her own placid and unremarkable way.

Her mood evidently softened slightly by her favourite birthday food, Gerda became more talkative as the meal ended.

"Of course, we get lumbered both ways," she remarked thoughtfully, eyeing a last morsel of fruit trifle. "With Dad, I mean. He's not only a doctor, which makes him so busy and all that, but he's a missionary as well—and that really puts the lid on it!"

"How do you mean?" Yasmin asked uneasily.

Gerda shrugged.

"Don't you see? A doctor has to do his best for his patients, of course, but when he's a missionary as well it's ten times worse. I mean, he's got to be even more self-sacrificing and—and loving his neighbour and all that. Ordinary humans like us, his family, don't stand a chance."

"But—if you're really a Christian that's what you want to do—love your neighbour, and so on," Yasmin protested.

"Do you? Honestly now, Yas," Gerda asked with the bluntness with which she often disconcerted people. " 'Cos I can tell you now, I jolly well don't. I don't mind folk I like, people who are decent to me, but I'm not awfully interested in those I don't know and I couldn't care less about strangers and people I don't like. Be honest now, Yas. Do you?"

Basically truthful, Yasmin hesitated, torn between what training and instinct told her she ought to be and her real feelings. In the end truth won.

"N-no, I suppose I don't care, really," she said slowly, her eyes widening in dismay as she thought it out, "and —Gerda, that's a bit grim. It means we're not Christians at all really. We're sort of—hypocrites."

"Exactly," Her sister nodded. "I'm not going on like it, either; not any longer. Just because we happen to be the daughters of a missionary it doesn't mean we have to believe like he does. I don't feel Christian in that way and I'm not the slightest bit interested in religion anyway, so I'm not going to pretend any more. I shall tell Dad when he does come in, so there."

"He'll be awfully upset," Yasmin said worriedly.

"I can't help that." Gerda sounded determined. "Another thing, I'm fed up with this place, with being stuck out here miles from anywhere. I want to go to a decent town and see a bit of life."

"What kind of life?" her sister asked reasonably, abandoning the more serious issue for the moment.

"Oh, I don't know; but there must be something more to it all than—than tea bushes and monsoons—and that's about all we ever see here. Do you realize we've only ever been in a proper car twice in all our lives—and I can't even remember seeing a train!"

"That was ages ago when we went down to that conference in Delhi. You did see a train, all right, even if you've forgotten it. I remember you yelled 'cos the noise scared you. And you were sick in the car coming back," Yasmin remembered.

"Well, even going just somewhere different would make a change," Gerda countered, moving restlessly over to the windows. "I hate being couped up here with just acres of tea plantations and scrub and bush and nothing else for miles and miles. What's more, I'm going to tell Dad so. He's got his job and he's busy so he enjoys it, but I don't and I think it's high time we had a chance to do what we want. You know, go places and have fun like other girls do. I've always wanted to skate and ski or be a champion swimmer ..."

"You swim here," Yasmin reminded her.

"Oh, that!" Her sister's small nose wrinkled disparagingly. "In a poky little pool and with no real competition." She looked at the older girl, half impatient, half curious. "Yas, be honest, do you really like living here? Isn't there anything you'd rather do?"

Yasmin caught her breath on a sharp sigh and gave in.

"Of course I'd much rather do lots of things," she admitted, "only this has always been our home and there's Dad's work and—"

"...and we don't know any better so we're supposed to be content and stick it out; grin and bear it," Gerda

9

finished for her. She caught at her sister's arm eagerly. "Yas, we don't have to put up with it now. We're grown up—well, almost, anyway. It's time we considered our future and I'm sure Dad will see it that way when we put it to him—"

"Oh, no, we couldn't do that. He'd be so awfully hurt—"

"...he'd be a lot more hurt if we got so fed up that we ran away." Gerda cut short the protest bluntly. "Yes, I mean it, Yas," she went on as Yasmin looked horrified. "This place gives me the jimjams and I shan't stick it much longer. I'm fourteen now and I'm going to speak up for myself, whatever you chose to do, so there."

"I'm with you, only, Gerda, do be careful what you say to Dad. It—it would be awful to hurt him," Yasmin pleaded, as always, shrinking from anything that might upset her father.

"'Course I'll be careful, what do you take me for?" Gerda was indignant. She pushed her short curly hair back from her face with an impatient gesture yet looked completely determined. "I'm not hurting anyone but I want *out*. In any case, haven't I any rights? Dad doesn't seem to bother about hurting me; he did promise most faithfully he'd come home early today."

"Something must have cropped up. He wouldn't forget a promise."

"Then he should have sent a message," Gerda said quite implacably and that seemed to be the last word on the subject.

She turned away and began moving restlessly about the long, low sitting-room while Yasmin curled up on a sofa and began to daydream about what life could be like somewhere else. She had never told anyone about those daydreams but her favourite one was based on the vague memory of her grandmother's home in distant Cornwall. There the big house stood in a lovely garden backed by tall pine trees, and a little winding path led between flowery bushes down to a bay where the sea foamed and creamed about the rocks that sheltered a beach of fine golden sand. There were tiny rock pools there and fascinating small creatures scurrying away from her bare toes as she paddled gently in the sun-warmed water. If she closed her eyes Yasmin could make herself believe she could hear the hiss and rustle of the sea and feel the soft breeze on her face. She wondered if her mother had ever longed for the home where she was born. Her father had come from Cornwall, too, and the only picture on the wall of his consulting room was of a small church on a clifftop above a rocky shore.

"Perhaps that's why we've got this yen to go there, Gerda and me," she thought dreamily, and then sat up with a jerk. "What's that?"

"Trouble." Gerda ran out on to the verandah and leaned over the rail to look down the road. In the distance, but coming closer with every moment a confused noise of wailing and human voices disturbed the quiet air. "Someone's had an accident, I expect, and everyone's dashing to the Clinic to find Dad, as usual."

Yasmin joined her sister at the rail, listening to the din that was rapidly growing louder. Then as the crowd evidently turned down the dusty side track that led to the Clinic both girls shrugged slightly and went indoors again without speaking, resigned to the fact that Dr. Oake would be home even later than ever now.

Although she said nothing Gerda's expression was very eloquent as she went to put a disc on the record-player, and it was quite clear to Yasmin that this latest development was hardening the younger girl's determination to rebel against their situation. For herself, she had to admit inwardly that Gerda had only said aloud what she had been thinking secretly for some time: neither of them had any real interest in their father's twin professions of missionary and doctor.

"I suppose it would be better to be honest about it and tell Dad," she was just thinking as hurried footsteps pattered along the verandah.

The door opened and Loti, Dr. Oake's young assistant, stood panting on the threshold.

"Dr. Sahib very ill," he said jerkily. "You come—please."

Accident

2
    "IS HE GOING TO DIE?" GERDA HARDLY RECOG-
nised her own voice, so hushed and croaky was its tone.

"No, of course not." Yasmin spoke with more haste than
real conviction. "He'll be all right after Dr. Southgate's
seen him. It's a good thing Loti and Sari between them
knew enough to set his broken leg, anyway."

"But Loti says he was ill and that's why he fell and broke
it." Gerda, restless as ever, fidgeted by the window. "If
only the doctor would come! It must be ages since he got
the message."

"Dr. Southgate's got to drive nearly 200 miles," Yasmin
pointed out. "He can't possibly get here much before six
this evening. Loti says Dad's c-comfortable."

Gerda came to fling a hasty arm about her sister, knowing that the older girl was just as upset and frightened as
she herself was, and they huddled together for comfort
on the hard bench in the Clinic's waiting-room. They had
been there all night, ever since Loti had brought the news
to their bungalow and although Sari and the other staff
had brought in camp beds for the two girls to rest on
neither had slept for more than a few catnaps during the
long dark hours.

At the back of the one-storey building Dr. Oake lay
only semi-conscious and obviously desperately ill in addition to having a broken leg, sustained when he had collapsed on the hillside on his way back from an emergency

case. Loti had been a tower of strength to the frightened sisters, sending his brother off in a jeep borrowed from Leolali's only owner of transport to the nearest hospital for help. The young Indian medical assistant had done the best with his limited knowledge and had at least made the patient more comfortable but it was clear even to Gerda's inexperienced eyes that Dr. Oake needed much more than first aid.

"Yas, I—I do feel awful," she said now after a pause. "He—Dad must have been lying out there wh - when I was binding because he hadn't come home for my b - birthday tea. If—if God only lets him get better I promise I won't grouse so m - much, honestly."

"I expect you will—we both will," Yasmin said with a flash of insight, "but we'll try harder not to, anyhow."

Sari and the ayah came in just then with comforting hot drinks for the two girls and they were persuaded to go out on to the verandah for a change of scene if nothing else.

It was a long and dreary day, one that neither girl was to forget. There was nothing they could do for their father, except pray, and neither could settle down to do anything else. Gerda at least found even prayer difficult enough since her rebellious thoughts had lately helped her to convince herself that although God probably did exist there was nothing to show that prayer was of any use.

Besides, she was troubled by her own sense of fairness so that it seemed hardly honest to her to doubt God and yet still to ask for His help. Less confused than her sister, Yasmin could only pray inarticulately for courage. As always she shrank from sickness and suffering and without being told she knew her father to be seriously ill. In spite of the heat of the day, there seemed to be an icy lump of dread inside her that nothing was able to dispel.

14

From mid-afternoon both girls hovered on the verandah, listening and watching with painful eagerness for the returning jeep. By 5 p.m. even placid Sari and Loti himself were taking turns in coming out to stare down the dusty track. It came at last, just when Gerda was deciding that she could bear the suspense no longer.

"It's coming—it's coming—oh, no! There's no one with him. Kala's alone!" cried Yasmin as the jeep came into view and they could see Loti's brother alone at the wheel. "Dr. Southgate hasn't come."

"There's another car." Gerda's quick hearing caught the sound of a second vehicle although the noise of its engine was almost swamped by the deafening clatter coming from the ancient jeep. Next moment a Land Rover appeared some way behind the jeep's dust cloud and a few minutes later both vehicles were drawn up outside the Clinic. Before the girls had time to say anything Dr. Southgate was coming to the verandah, followed by another man and a tall, fair girl.

"Girls, this is a colleague, Dr. Ward. Where's the patient? Loti, lead the way."

"You poor lambs, don't look so shattered. We're all here to help." The fair girl put a friendly arm about Yasmin who was shaking in sudden relief, and smiled at Gerda. "You won't know me. I'm Anne Southgate. Mother couldn't come herself because my kid brothers are at home and it's one person's full-time job keeping them out of mischief. As soon as Father says it's safe to move your Dad we're taking him out and Dr. Ward will stay to run the Clinic. You two are coming home with me. Now, while the medics are attending to their patient suppose you show me your bungalow and we'll start thinking about some packing."

Under her gentle but firm influence the juniors were kept busy for the next hour or so.

"We're flying your father out now," Dr. Southgate explained as soon as he was able to leave his patient in Dr. Ward's temporary care. "There's an army helicopter coming over for him soon and he'll be taken to hospital. Anne will stay here with you for tonight and then tomorrow she'll take you to our home. I shall travel with your father, of course. Anne will help you to pack up your personal things so that Dr. Ward can take over here as well as at the Clinic."

"It—it's awfully kind of you all," stammered Yasmin, looking as bewildered as she felt, "but—but is it O.K. for Dr. Ward to stay? I mean, we don't know how long it will be before we're back and—," she halted uncertainly as Dr. Southgate exchanged a glance with his daughter.

"You won't be coming back, Yasmin," the doctor said quietly. "Evidently your father did not have time to tell you of his plans. I believe he was keeping it as a surprise for Gerda's birthday. You see, he has known for some time that he was unwell—which is why we were well prepared for today's emergency. He was only waiting for Dr. Ward to be ready to take over here so that he could return to England with you."

"To England!" Such a host of mixed emotions welled up in the sisters that neither knew whether to laugh or cry, and guessing a little of what they felt Anne hurried to add more explanations.

"Yes; we understand that when your grandmother died a few years ago she left her home to her only son, Dr. Oake. At present your Aunt Elizabeth is living there, but it's a large house, apparently, and your Dad has been arranging for you all to go and share it with her. That way,

16

you'll have a proper home and be able to finish your education properly. Now—is that the 'copter, Dad?"

It was, and in the sudden flurry to dash down to the only patch of cleared ground near the Clinic there was no time to discuss the stupendous news they had been told. If they had not been so worried and anxious about their father, lying so white-faced and still on the stretcher, the girls would have been dancing for joy. But with Dr. Oake looking like that and barely able to whisper their names both Yasmin and Gerda were too upset and tearful to think of pleasant things.

"Chins up, girls." Dr. Southgate gave them a heartening smile before climbing into the helicopter after his patient. "With good nursing and care we'll soon have him well again, please God. 'Bye, Anne-girl. Take care of yourself and mind how you drive tomorrow."

The little group consisting of Dr. Ward, Loti, Sari, Anne and the sisters stood back in the scrubby grassland as the helicopter roared up and away, and watched until it was a tiny black speck in the distance. Then Gerda heaved a sigh that seemed to come all the way from her sandals.

"Poor old Dad, he won't even be able to enjoy the journey," she said, blinking hard at the tears that would come in spite of her determination.

Yasmin rubbed the back of her hand across her eyes and gave a watery grin.

"I don't suppose he's bothered about that. Come on, Gerda, there's a mass of things to do if we're leaving here tomorrow—and we haven't arranged Miss Southgate's room yet, either."

"Oh, please! Anne, not Miss Southgate," the older girl said quickly. "I shall feel positively ancient otherwise." She linked an arm in each of the girls' and walked them back to the bungalow chatting determinedly about the packing. Her juniors had had a considerable shock and with little sleep, food, or rest during the past twenty-four hours Anne knew that both were not far from collapse. The sooner she had them safely indoors and ready for bed the better for them, at present. Accordingly, she fairly bustled them about once they reached the bungalow, keeping them busy to such good effect that by the time they went to bed they were both physically tired enough to sleep without taking the tablets which Dr. Southgate had left with Anne as a precaution.

"Sleep's their best medicine at the moment," Dr. Ward agreed quietly, having come up to the bungalow later to check that all was well. "It's been a nasty knock for them but they've taken it well. The excitement of going home to England and the complete change will do the rest. By the time they realise that their father's going to be an invalid for some time to come they'll be better able to bear it."

"What is his condition?" Anne asked, nodding agreement.

"Serious but not critical. All the same, he has been a sick man for many months. I don't know how he has found the strength to keep going."

"His Grace is sufficient for me," quoted Anne softly. "Dad says it's Dr. Oake's faith in God that's enabled him to accomplish so much here. The amount of work he has done would have defeated a lesser man—or any man, without God's help."

"I agree with your father. I only hope my own faith will be equal to the challenge," Dr. Ward said, seriously, as he went back through the darkness to his temporary quarters in the Clinic.

After the stress and strain of the previous night and day,

the entire household slept late next morning and the sun was climbing high in the sky before everyone was awake and up.

"We'll have to put our skates on if we're to be home tonight," Anne said. "We've some fairly grim tracks to cover. I don't want to badger you, girls, but don't be too long in making your farewells, will you?"

"We won't," they chorused and certainly kept their word, Yasmin because she hated saying goodbye to people she liked and Gerda because she had had time to realise that her dearest wish was being granted and she was too excited about it to want to linger.

"Don't worry if you've forgotten to pack anything. Just send me a note and I'll see that everything is forwarded on to you," Dr. Ward assured them, and at last they were able to give a final hug and kiss to ayah and Sari, shake hands with Loti and a dozen other well-wishers before climbing into the Land Rover. With a fiercesome growl the engine started up and then they were rattling away in a cloud of dust.

"That's that," said Gerda with immense satisfaction. "No more living in the backwoods for me. Look out, World, here we come!"

"I wish we could have brought ayah and dear old Sari with us. Still, I suppose we can't have everything as we want it, even in the outside world," Yasmin said with a sigh, half regret, half satisfaction, and Anne chuckled aloud.

"Even *less* in the outside world can people have what they want," she commented, meeting their surprised looks. "The more people there are around, the more it is an art to learn to live with them, I'm afraid."

"We'll manage," Gerda declared confidently, while Yasmin looked doubtful. "I *like* a challenge."

Yasmin Speaks her Mind

3 "O.K. EVERYBODY OUT." ANNE SOUTHGATE
brought the Land Rover to a halt in the shade of a clump
of trees and nodded to her companions. Nothing loth, the
girls clambered out on to the hard dust track, thankful
to stretch themselves after hours of anything but smooth
travel. "Rake out the picnic basket, will you, Gerda, and
we'll have a snack. Wow! I'm stiff."

"Me, too, though you can't say we've been sitting still,
exactly," Gerda said, giggling a little. "We've rattled and
bounced like—like beans in a can."

"I'm glad Dad didn't have to come this way," Yasmin
said more seriously. "It would have hurt him so."

"It would indeed, which is why we used the helicopter
Here you are, girls, drink up. We can't stop too long at
present." Anne spoke briskly. While it was clear that
Gerda at least had almost recovered from the shock of her
father's collapse it was equally evident that Yasmin, more
thoughtful and sensitive, had taken the matter more
deeply. The younger girl, convinced that her father was in
safe hands and going to be made well, had turned all her
thoughts towards the excitement and pleasures in store for
her, while Yasmin was still bewildered by the suddenness
of the upheaval and unhappy about Dr. Oake.

"You two aren't much alike, are you?" Anne commented, following her own train of thought as the trio
carefully repacked the small picnic basket after refreshing

themselves with iced tea and fresh fruit. "In our family we're all monotonously the same in looks, although not in ways."

"Oh no. Gerda's the family beauty," Yasmin roused herself to explain. She looked at her sister without envy. "Loti and the rest used to call her the Golden One."

"I'm more nearly the Silver One now," Gerda herself laughed. "All the sun does is to bleach my hair till it's nearly white. I don't even sun-tan like Yas. She's really golden."

"Only my skin. My hair's plain mouse," Yasmin said. "When we get back to England I expect I'll simply look sallow and you'll go all honey colour again."

"England. Wow! I am looking forward to it," Gerda chattered eagerly as the three boarded the Land Rover again to continue the journey. Once they started off, however, the talk died away for the somewhat elderly vehicle rattled and banged and shuddered over the unsurfaced roads in a tornado of noise and dust so that conversation was almost impossible. Anne herself was beginning to feel tired with the strain of driving in the heavy airless heat. The scenery around was of no particular interest as they passed, miles and miles of scrub after they left the acres of tea bushes and then as the road wound down laboriously to the plains, wide, flat and almost bare, with the heat growing ever more noticeable.

"I shall be glad, glad, glad to see the back of all this," Gerda said fiercely when they made a second brief stop for refreshment later in the afternoon. "It's nothing but monotony and misery. I hate it."

"There's a great deal of beauty, too, if one looks for it," Anne told her quietly. "As for the misery, yes, there's much of that which is why people like your father and

21

mine are here. If enough is done to train and help a time will come when the poverty and sickness will be conquered and the people have the same good living standards as you and I enjoy."

Gerda looked a little rebellious, her pretty mouth stubborn.

"I know all that, but it doesn't make any difference as far as I'm concerned. I don't see why men like our fathers should give up their whole life—and often ruin their health —all for other people. Some of them aren't even a little bit grateful, either."

"Gerda, I wish you wouldn't say things like that," Yasmin protested, unhappily, but her sister shook the curly flaxen hair back from her face defiantly.

"Why not? It's the truth, and you know it. *I* wouldn't do it even if I were a doctor."

"Isn't that a rather selfish attitude?" Anne asked mildly, choosing her words carefully. Even in the short time she had been with the Oake girls she had come to realise that Gerda was the more difficult and slightly spoilt one.

"No, I don't think it is," the junior answered now, her deep brown eyes sparkling a little angrily. "I'm quite ready to help people I know, like—like relatives and friends. I'm not selfish. It's simply that I can't get all worried and anxious about total strangers and I'm not going to pretend I can, because that would be worse than selfish, it would be downright dishonest."

Yasmin was biting her lip nervously and looking distressed, but Anne was quite equal to the occasion and unruffled by Gerda's outburst.

"I quite agree that it would be dishonest to pretend," she said equably. "I hope you aren't suggesting that Dr. Oake, or my father, is dishonest? I wonder how you imagine they manage to care for so many strangers?"

Gerda looked taken aback and slightly confused but she rallied quickly.

"Well—they're—they're grown-up and—doctors and—of course I don't think they're dishonest," she added indignantly.

"Do you think caring for people is easier for grown-ups then?" Anne asked, concealing a smile and beginning to repack the picnic basket, helped by the silent Yasmin.

"It must be," Gerda said frankly, rinsing the beakers in one of the cans of water they carried with them.

Anne laughed, although she was feeling rather too weary to enjoy an argument at present.

"My dear girl, it most certainly is not, I can assure you."

"Then, why on earth do they bother?" Gerda dried the beakers and put them away with an impatient gesture.

"I'm sure you know why without my telling you, Gerda." Anne paused to look straitly at the young rebel and the latter's fair skin that seldom browned in sunshine flushed deeply red. Nevertheless, she met the older girl's look unhesitatingly.

"I suppose I do. It's because they're Christians. Well, I decided the other day that I'm not, so that's all there is to it."

Anne looked at her shrewdly, silently ushering her back into the Land Rover after Yasmin, who had hurriedly jumped aboard to avoid the argument.

"That's odd. I wouldn't have thought *you*'d have funked it," Anne said casually, and deliberately started the engine so that its usual deafening noise effectively put an end to the talk. There were still some sixty miles to be travelled before the party would reach the Southgate home and

Anne judged that she had given Gerda quite sufficient to think about for the moment. The elder girl guessed that her junior was a little proud as well as spoilt and, judging by the latter's look of boundless astonishment and indignation, her guess was correct. In fact, Gerda scarcely noticed the discomfort of the remaining journey since she was inwardly bubbling over with annoyance at the mere suggestion that she might be a coward.

Accustomed as she was to having a fairly comfortable opinion of herself and to being, because of her liveliness and good looks, something of a leader among other girls, Gerda's self-esteem had just received a considerable blow. Moreover, being unable to answer back at once was forcing her to consider the implications more deeply than she liked. The result being that by the time the Land Rover was running into the outskirts of a sizeable town she was beginning to wonder uneasily if she was, after all, rather scared of committing herself to being a Christian.

"I s'pose I am, in a way," she admitted inwardly, "but only because I've seen how—how dedicated Dad has had to be and really hard-working and—and I just don't think I could ever be like that. I like to have fun and enjoy life, and I'm sure that's not wrong, so there."

Next moment her attention was diverted by all the bustle and movement of the town as Anne drove carefully through narrow streets crowded with bullock-carts, bicycles, and pedestrians all moving along without much regard for any rule of the road. Lights were beginning to illumine the various small cave-like shops and the pungent spicy smells of Indian cooking wafted into the Land Rover from all sides. Slowly Anne threaded a way through the confusion and finally drove out on to a wider, less crowded road where a little apart from the town a modern hospital building stood with one or two small European-style bungalows close by.

The Land Rover came to a stop in front of the bungalow nearest to the hospital and as the sound of its engine died abruptly a plump fair-haired woman came out on to the narrow terrace, followed by Dr. Southgate himself.

"Home sweet home," Anne said unnecessarily. "Hop out, girls, we've arrived. Hi, Dad, Mother. Told you we'd manage it if the old crate didn't collapse en route."

"She's no beauty, I know, but she is reliable," Dr. Southgate said in mock protest, with a kindly eye for the two juniors who looked tired and suddenly rather apprehensive as they realised that now they would have more news of their father. "Come along in, girls. I don't think we'll disturb your father tonight as he is resting quietly just now. But you'll be able to see him early tomorrow, I promise you."

"Oh good! That's all right then," Gerda said with her usual carelessness, but Yasmin's dark eyes looked anxiously at the doctor.

"He—he's all right, isn't he?" she asked fearfully.

"He is quite ill and at the moment very tired but he is resting and beginning to respond to treatment," the doctor answered fairly, and glanced at his wife who rose to the occasion at once.

"Now come indoors, Yasmin and—Gerda, is it? Yes, come along, then, and make yourselves at home. We've put you together in the room next to Anne's."

Keeping up a gentle flow of conversation Mrs. Southgate led the way indoors and was soon showing them the pleasant airy bedroom set aside for visitors. They were both tired and hot and glad enough to have a refreshing shower and change into clean clothes before joining the family in the dining-room. Here they were introduced to Kevin and Keith, Anne's young twin brothers, and Gerda, at least, was soon chattering away happily as she ate a good meal. Yasmin ate less and was rather silent except when the Southgates drew her into the conversation. The truth was that the older Oake girl was for the first time in her life feeling homesick. Much as she had, like her sister, chafed against the isolation of their situation up in the hills above Leolali, the sudden upheaval and the unexpected uprooting from all that was familiar and home had left Yasmin shaken and uncertain of herself. Her father was seriously ill, she and Gerda were homeless at present and, however kind and hospitable the Southgates were, the future seemed very dark and rather frightening to Yasmin that evening.

"Isn't this a pretty wizard place after Leolali?" chattered Gerda cheerfully later, as the girls prepared for bed. "I'm going to have a good buzz around the bazaar tomorrow. 'Course, it's not much like a real town but it'll do till we get to England anyway. How soon do you reckon we'll be going there, Yas?"

Normally Yasmin was a peaceable soul who took most of her sister's ways without criticism or complaint but, tired as she was after the long day's journey and upset about her father, this time Gerda's attitude struck her as being totally selfish and quite indefensible.

"I don't know and I don't care," Yasmin said with sudden passionate intensity. "Can't you think of anything else but what *you* want? What about poor Dad, lying there ill? How can you be so selfish?"

Caught off guard, Gerda's ready temper flared, fuelled by the inner knowledge that she was being just as selfish as Yasmin had declared. Unfortunately, the inner knowledge

26

did not help to mend matters and suddenly all the old rebellious feelings came uppermost.

"O.K. So I'm selfish because I'm honest enough to say what I think," she flared. "Of course I'm sorry for Dad but I'm not one of your mealy-mouthed Sunday School types to pretend to be unhappy all the time. I can't help Dad by being miserable."

For once Yasmin made no attempt to coax her sister into a more reasonable mood. Instead, she simply stared at her for a moment and then quietly finished her preparations before kneeling as usual to say her bedtime prayers. Uncomfortably, Gerda hesitated before, with a defiant shrug, she climbed into her bed and lay down. An uneasy silence fell.

A Job for Ann

4

"DO YOU MEAN *NOW*, AT ONCE?"

"But why can't we go with him? Why have we got to wait?"

The second speaker was Gerda, of course, never one to be patient about anything.

"Because special arrangements have been made for your father. He has to travel on a stretcher, remember," Mrs. Southgate pointed out. "It isn't every flight that can accommodate an invalid like that." She looked up from her pastry making and met Yasmin's big worried eyes. At once her expression became very kindly although her voice was still calm and matter of fact. "The sooner Dr. Oake can be flown to England the sooner he will be on the road to recovery, Yasmin. The hospital here is not equipped to give him all the special treatment that he needs, in fact the treatment which he must have if he is to get well. So, you see, it's very fortunate that a flight can take him so quickly. You won't mind when you know it's for his benefit, will you?"

"N-no, only it—he'll be so far away," Yasmin said rather dismally. "I hoped we could have travelled with him."

"Yes, we would all have liked that for you," Mrs. Southgate agreed. "However, it isn't possible and we must do the very best for the patient as you know."

"We know," said both sisters, although the tone of

28

Gerda's voice sounded anything but resigned to the situation. However, she had the good sense not to make any further comment, thinking that her rebellious feelings would find little sympathy in a household where personal sacrifice and selflessness were the accepted way of life. Dr. and Mrs. Southgate had been medical missionaries even longer than Dr. and Mrs. Oake. Nevertheless, the girls had not spent their first week with the Southgate family without their elders learning quite a lot about them, and Mrs. Southgate understood more than the young rebel realised. Accordingly she sent Yasmin off into the dining-room with a handful of cutlery to place on the table and then looked at Gerda with a smile.

"Making sacrifices isn't easy, is it, Gerda?"

The junior looked up sharply from the piece of scrap dough she was twisting in her fingers.

"No, it isn't, and—and I don't see why we should keep on having to make 'em," she said bluntly, encouraged by the understanding in Mrs. Southgate's face.

"Everyone wonders that from time to time and there's never a clear answer if we think only of ourselves. It's what is right for the other person that's often the real answer. Here, Gerda, roll out that bit of pastry and then you can make it into a pop-over; I've some apples you can put inside it."

Intrigued by the novelty of doing a little cooking, something she had never done at home since the ayah had always prepared the family meals and had not encouraged the girls to come into her kitchen, Gerda forgot that she was beginning to resent a mild lecture and began to roll out the pastry with great care. Mrs. Southgate put the finishing touches to the pie she was making and put it into the oven. By the time Gerda's own efforts had been placed on a baking sheet and also put in the oven the junior had lost most of her resentment.

"That's that. Do you know, Mrs. Southgate, that's the first pop-over I've ever made. I hope it turns out all right." She looked at her hostess frankly. "Yas told me the other day that I was selfish—and I suppose she's right but—but I can't pretend to love other people more than myself because I don't and I can't see that I ever will."

"Very few of us do, if we are honest about it, and certainly it must be one of the hardest things in the world even to attempt on one's own."

Gerda shrugged a little.

"Oh, I know what you're going to say now—the good old stock answer: love God and you'll want to love everyone else. I've heard it all hundreds of times. Don't forget, Dad's a missionary, too. But it just doesn't work with me, that's all."

"It doesn't work, as you call it, with anyone unless they really try to follow the Saviour," Mrs. Southgate pointed out. "You do believe in God, I take it?"

"Oh yes. Well, I mean it stands to reason that someone must have started everything in the beginning," Gerda admitted fairly. "All the wonderful things scientists discover today must have been put there for them first, otherwise they couldn't find out about them now. But believing in God doesn't really help me much, Mrs. Southgate. I mean, I know He made me and all that and I'm grateful but it doesn't make me want to go all mushy over everyone else."

Her hostess chuckled, liking the young rebel's honesty if not her sentiments.

"I somehow think that you have quite the wrong idea about the meaning of loving someone, quite apart from

30

anything else," she said. "Oh, don't worry, I'm not going to preach you a sermon. I imagine you've heard many. Just let me say this—get to know Jesus Himself and you will want to do as He wants. Once you do that you'll find even the things you dislike most become bearable and sometimes almost easy to do. Now, let's go and see how Yasmin is getting on with laying the table, shall we?"

Gerda was glad enough to end the talk for, kindly as it had been, it still was a grown-up lecture and therefore thoroughly boring to anyone as impatient and opinionated as the younger Oake girl. Nevertheless, as with many wise talks, a little of it would be remembered later and better understood.

Now, however, Gerda was more pleased to be helping with practical things and particularly eager to see whether her first attempt at cooking was a success.

The Oake girls had been guests at the Southgate home for eight days now and although the doctor had said little they knew that their father had not made any real progress towards recovery during that time. In common with many other devoted and dedicated men he had carried on with his work for far longer than had been advisable and was now paying the penalty of having a more difficult struggle to recover his own health. Hence the decision to send him to England on the very first available flight. Naturally the girls had expected to travel with him and the news that he was to go alone while they awaited a later flight had disappointed them both badly. Inevitably, Gerda had taken the situation less calmly, but even Yasmin's normally placid acceptance of things had been shaken. She reacted less violently than her sister, nevertheless her doubts were just as strong, although not so self-centered as Gerda's.

"It doesn't seem really fair, does it?" she remarked to Anne Southgate as the latter escorted her juniors home from the hospital where they had been spending a short time with Dr. Oake who was due to fly to England in three days' time. "I mean, Daddy's worked for God for years and years and now he's ill. Yet, lots of people don't even think of God or do anything for Him and they're O.K."

"I don't think fairness comes into it," Anne said thoughtfully. "I'm no expert to explain these things, but I do know that if we all got what we deserved in life with complete fairness some of us would be in a bit of a tizzy! Seriously though, Yasmin, I don't think your father thinks his illness is unfair. After all, he chose to work out here, no one, least of all God, said that he had to, or that he had to work so hard that he became ill. And you know, I think he's quite happy and cheerful in spite of everything. I certainly haven't heard him grumble, have you?"

"Oh no, he wouldn't," Yasmin agreed.

"Well then, don't get it into your head that he's being treated unfairly or punished in some way, or that God is to blame for his illness," Anne said bluntly having, as she told her mother later, some difficulty in coping with the sisters' moods and questions. She was not very much older than Yasmin and had always had a happy unquestioning faith since childhood so that although she knew and trusted her Saviour she found it less easy to explain her personal convictions to the juniors. Nevertheless, the girl's question did make her pause to examine her own beliefs and, as Mrs. Southgate pointed out, it is no bad thing to be jolted out of complacency at times.

"Ouch! I deserved that, I suppose." Anne gave her mother an affectionate hug. "O.K. I'll try to help the kids although they do *deave* me at times, and Gerda certainly is just one big question mark at the moment. And anyone knows I'm no theologian. I haven't the brains for it."

"No, but you are a disciple, a follower, which is more important and we are all called to teach where we can," her mother reminded her quietly. "Those two girls are at a crisis in their lives and it's possible that what they understand and think now may affect their whole futures."

Anne looked serious at this.

"You're not expecting Dr. Oake to recover enough to take a grip on things for some time then," she said shrewdly. "H'm. If that's so, I do see that it's important for them to get straightened out now or anything might happen. Gerda's quite a rebel already I would think, and of course we don't know what kind of a person their aunt is in England, although she's Dr. Oake's sister so she ought to be O.K."

"She is also a widow and may be bitter about her circumstances," Mrs. Southgate added. "However, as you will be travelling back to England with the girls, at least you'll have that much more time to influence them for good."

"It's a pity we're not going by boat, then. A jet plane doesn't leave you much time," Anne grinned. "Don't worry, Mother, I'll do my best. They're not bad kids and I'd hate to see them getting wrong ideas about the things that really matter. All the same, I had no idea I'd be conducting a private Sunday School this vac!"

She had no idea either of a number of other unusual things she would be doing before her holiday ended. In fact, had she been able to see into the future Anne would certainly not have felt so cheerfully unconcerned about her return journey to England where she was due to begin her final year at university before taking up a career in radiology. Neither would Yasmin and Gerda have been so impatient to join their own flight to Europe. Fortunately, for the girls' peace of mind, however, they could all know only the present and that was full of activity.

First, Dr. Oake's departure was unexpectedly put forward so that he was able to be flown to England two whole days before the original date fixed. It was all so sudden that to the girls it seemed almost dreamlike, just a hurried journey from the hospital to the airport in an ambulance, a quick hug and kiss for the pale-faced invalid, and then their father was being whisked away on a comfortable stretcher and finally disappearing into the silver fuselage of a jet plane.

Not that they were given much time to brood over the separation. The Southgate household was a busy one especially as now when the junior members of the family were at home for the holidays. Kevin and Keith, Anne's young brothers, were a lively and entertaining pair who, when they were not experimenting with their idea of scientific theories, were not lacking in fertile imagination and usually managed to fall into mischief at least once every day.

A cable from England announcing Dr. Oake's safe arrival further cheered the girls and then, quite suddenly, it was their turn and they were driving to the airport with Anne en route to join their own flight.

"Well, you can't say this isn't an adventure, Yas," Gerda said gleefully. "Bullock-cart to jet plane is a real jump forward. Aren't you thrilled?"

"I will be—when we arrive safely." Yasmin was more cautious. "I think I'm happier with my feet on the ground."

The Flight

5

"Isn't this really something? Super, I call it. Wouldn't you agree!"

It was Gerda, of course, thrilled to the marrow at being airborne and high above the hot parched land. Yasmin was taking longer to adjust to the new sensation of flying.

"This is only a relief plane," Anne was telling the other girl. "It takes us to Delhi and then we board one of the really big jets to take us all the rest of the way to England. That's why this one is half empty, I suppose."

Yasmin nodded, trying her best to look as if she were enjoying the rather bumpy flight.

"Let's hope we get a smoother ride in the other plane," Gerda grunted suddenly as the aircraft jolted and dipped rather alarmingly.

"Sure to," Anne said rather absently, looking a trifle puzzled. "That's odd. I don't remember flying over such hilly country when I came out."

"Perhaps we're taking a different route because it's a smaller plane," Gerda volunteered.

"Could be." Nevertheless Anne still looked disconcerted.

The plane was indeed one of the smaller aircraft used on short internal flights and at present only carried eight other passengers besides the three girls. Most of these looked like business men, and the remainder were a party of two boys and a girl apparently en route to school after their holidays.

Unaccountably restive, Anne looked along the cabin to where the little Indian stewardess stood. It struck the English girl that there was an air of tension about the air hostess and even as she registered the thought one of the two passengers who had gone forward a little earlier reappeared abruptly from the flight deck. Suddenly it was obvious that he was no ordinary business man. In one hand was a wicked looking revolver. He rapped out an order and prodded the air hostess sharply. Nervously she translated his words into the English understood by most of the passengers.

"He says this is a hi-jack. If everyone will keep calm and quiet no one will be hurt. They do not wish to hurt."

Stunned, the English girls looked at one another and around the cabin. Quite clearly, four of the soberly dressed men were in league with the gunman. His companion was presumably guarding and directing the pilot, and two others had risen in their seats, smiling and joking with the gunman. Apart from the school children only one other, a young Sikh, was apparently a genuine passenger. The hi-jacking had been well planned, Anne guessed, for these small inter-airport planes were seldom crowded and carried only the minimum crew.

"Wow! How's this for an adventure?" murmured Gerda, but her voice sounded a little hollow even to herself.

"It's one I could well do without," Anne said rather tartly. "We may land up anywhere now they've taken over. We certainly won't make our connection at Delhi in time. I *thought* we'd changed course."

Whatever she might be feeling inwardly her voice only sounded annoyed at the disruption of the flight and insensibly the children's fears subsided. One of the boys managed a rather shaky grin and the other nodded.

"Anyway, we'll be jolly late for school and that will give me time to finish my holiday essay," he said with a fairly good effort at jauntiness.

Not to be outdone by younger and smaller children even if they were boys, Yasmin pulled herself together.

"I'm glad it's us they've hi-jacked and not Dad," she said with more earnestness than good English. "It won't hurt us but it could have made him even more ill if they had delayed getting him to the hospital."

Reassured that the hi-jacking only meant delay, the boys' sister forgot how frightened she had been of the gunman, and managed a wobbly smile at Anne and her party. The young Sikh obviously understood English and glanced speculatively from one to the other before, apparently reassured by their calm, he went back to reading his book.

"Where will they take us, do you think, Anne?" Yasmin asked a little later. With the exception of the Sikh the men were all talking earnestly in their own language and the air hostess was busy with the other children.

"It's hard to say, Yasmin." Anne was frowning thoughtfully. "This is such a small plane and I doubt if it carries much spare fuel. I don't know much about these things but I wouldn't have thought we could go very far. I suppose, roughly the same distance as it is to Delhi only in the opposite direction, north eastwards."

"Towards Nepal and the mountains, then." Gerda, tried to remember her geography and the map. "Wow! Do you think they're making for Tibet or—or China?"

"If they are they'll never make it in this crate," Anne said with some asperity for it seemed quite likely to her that the hi-jackers might well be aiming for such a destina-

37

tion. "They'll be absolutely crazy to try it. I would have thought even they would realise this plane's too small—especially without refuelling."

"It—it won't be very nice if we run out of fuel and c-come down in the mountains," Yasmin said shakily and Gerda swallowed hard, her face paling.

"The understatement of the year," Anne commented calmly, although her own face was rather white. She slipped an arm into Yasmin's and managed a brief reassuring smile at Gerda. "Still, I don't suppose the men want to crash either, so they'll probably bring us down long before the fuel runs out."

"There's that, of course." Gerda's face brightened. "They can't sort of abandon ship, can they? I mean, we're all stuck up here together and it's just as risky for them as for us."

"That's it. We're all in this together, and God is with us all the time," Anne said firmly. "And now, I'm going to ask Him specially to take care of us and I suggest you do the same. Then we'll play 'I spy' for a while and ask those boys and their sister to join in."

Even Gerda had no disagreement with either of those suggestions and for the next few moments all three girls closed their eyes and prayed silently and very earnestly for help and courage in their present situation.

"Right. Now we've done all we can," Anne said briskly, opening her eyes. "Ask those three to join us, Gerda, and we'll start playing. Yasmin, you begin."

For the next hour she kept the five children firmly concentrating on 'I spy' and paper games while the plane droned on over increasingly wild country. The hi-jackers eyed them curiously at times but were apparently content to see them occupied peaceably and giving no trouble.

That the men had problems of their own was obvious to Anne who kept a wary eye on their activities as they came and went between the flight deck and cabin. Discussions and arguments were soon taking place and although Anne did not know the dialect enough to understand the conversation she did gather enough to know that the fuel situation was the main subject under discussion.

"H'm. It's just dawned on 'em," Gary, the elder of the two boy passengers, said scornfully. He glanced up at Anne quickly. "You were right, we haven't enough juice to go as far as they want."

Anne bit her lip, wishing the junior had not understood the men's conversation, for his sister and the Oake girls were looking uneasy again.

"Then I expect we shall land somewhere quite soon," she said with a calm she was far from feeling, and insisted on continuing the game they were playing.

Nevertheless it was a frightening situation. The aircraft was flying over thickly wooded hillsides with almost no open ground visible at all. Anne guessed that they were somewhere over Nepal, going towards the massive mountains of the Himalayas, of which these below were some of the lower foothills. It was a wild and rugged country with only a scattering of tiny hamlets and villages to break the pattern of rocks and trees. Clearly the hi-jackers had miscalculated in picking this particular plane for their use and now a tremendous argument was going on about it.

Outwardly serene, Anne was inwardly praying quite desperately that no one would do anything to make a dangerous situation more lethal and judging by their expressive faces her juniors were doing the same. In spite of the surface calm, the atmosphere was steadily growing more tense with every moment as the men argued back and forth.

Finally they seemed to come to a decision. One went through to the flight deck once more while the rest sat silent. Presently he returned, nodded curtly at the others and spoke to the stewardess whose big eyes widened nervously as she listened intently. Then, with a little bow of acknowledgement, she came towards the passengers.

"Now for it," muttered Gerda, and Yasmin gripped her sister's hand hard.

"The pilot has been instructed to land soon," she said in her clear English with its clipped accent. "Then he will take the men on to where they wish. Do not be alarmed, please. We shall not be too far from a village. The pilot knows the country well."

There was little they could say, everyone guessing that protest would be useless and even dangerous.

"It looks like we're going to have a long, long walk back," Gary said rather hollowly.

"Still, if we're going to be abandoned I'd much rather be on the ground," Gerda said with conviction, and Yasmin nodded agreement.

"I think the pilot must have persuaded those men not to take us any further, don't you, Anne?" she said. "Decent of him, because I suppose he'll have to go on with them. I wonder if the stewardess is coming with us or staying with them."

No one answered her for the plane at that moment made a sudden jolting dip to port and for the next few minutes the flight was far too bumpy to be enjoyable. Ridge after ridge of wooded hills had been rolling away to the horizon on every side and nowhere did there ever seem to be even a small area of flat land on which an aircraft could land.

Now, however, the foothills had given way to lofty mountains separated by deep narrow valleys, along one of which the plane was at present flying, and even less did there seem any possibility of landing. The girls held their breath as the dark walls of rock and forest rose up more closely on either side. The trees were knotted and gnarled, with bunches of moss hanging like beards from their trunks and branches. Great gashes scarred the mountainsides where the summer monsoon had washed away enormous chunks of earth and rock and one could see the path the debris had taken as it crashed down into the turbulent river at the bottom of the gorge. A kind of numbness seemed to settle on all the passengers as the uneasy flight continued and shreds and wisps of mist appeared laced among the trees while the hard, bright sunlight had vanished into grey gloom. Then suddenly the stewardess pointed and what Anne had at first sight thought to be another landslide scar could now be seen as a long narrow and fairly level clearing ahead, across the end of the valley.

It seemed pitifully tiny amid the vast bulk of the mountains but evidently it was the landing strip the pilot intended using. He brought the aircraft round in a gentle curve, losing height gradually, and then, almost abruptly, the ground seemed to rush nearer and they were down and taxiing along a rough and rutted surface.

"We must hurry, please. Take all your luggage. The pilot must not wait long."

The passengers did not need much encouragement to hurry although the world outside the aircraft hardly looked inviting. But the hi-jackers were looking impatient and the gunman was obviously much less patient than the rest. Accordingly, Anne and her juniors were soon standing on the rocky ground while the men threw out the rest of their luggage. The stewardess handed out a bundle of blankets from the emergency store and finally clambered down to join them, clutching sundry bags and a large water container. At once the gunman closed the door and everyone stood well back as the plane taxiied away and turned to take off again.

"What about the other man—the Sikh?" asked Anne quickly, and the stewardess shook her head.

"He chose to stay. The pilot is his brother," she said simply before, with a deafening roar, the plane took off and swept away, climbing steadily into the grey sky.

They watched breathlessly as it seemed to go closer and closer to the mountain wall before slipping sharply sideways and out eastwards through a gap between two massive peaks. The sound of the engines faded and soon there was only the noise of distant water, the whistle of a biting wind through the trees, and the stranded travellers were alone on the airstrip.

Stranded

6

"WELL, WH - WHAT DO WE DO NOW?" AS USUAL Gerda was the first to speak, although her voice was decidedly wobbly.

"Light a fire, that's for sure," Anne said with determination. "This wind's cold and, anyway, it'll show the villagers where we are."

"Are we going to stay here?" Yasmin sounded as if she did not know whether to laugh or cry. Unexpectedly the little stewardess answered her with great firmness.

"Yes, it is important that we stay here. We must make a camp and in time we shall be rescued. Here are matches and we have food and blankets."

"Right. Good practice for when you're Girl Guides," Anne said briskly. "By the way, shall we be introduced? What do we call you, Miss—er—?"

"My Christian name is Aban," said the stewardess, smiling. "You, I know, are Miss Southgate, and these are Yasmin and Gerda Oake, yes? And Gary, Jonathan and Heather Northcott. Good; now we make camp."

Thankful to be busy, everyone scouted around for suitable firewood among the scrubby bushes. Keeping a wary eye on her juniors, Anne moved closer to where Aban was breaking off some stunted azalea twigs.

"Was the pilot able to tell you how far we are from a village, Aban?"

Like Anne, Aban glanced swiftly towards the children before speaking in low tones.

"Yes, he was, Miss Southgate ..."

"Anne," the English girl interposed firmly. "We're all in this together."

"Anne, then; thank you." Aban smiled. "The village is one day's walk from here but the people will have seen the plane come down and will be sure to come to us soon. They will be excited, you see. Visitors are rare here and they will come, so we must wait."

"Just as well," Anne said decidedly. "I wouldn't fancy trekking through this country without a guide."

"No, indeed, we should soon be lost and in real danger." City-bred Aban gave a little shiver as she glanced around. "Come, we have enough for a fire now."

"There's a flat rock here; wouldn't it do for a fireplace?" Gerda and Gary came racing up with their arms full of twigs, followed by Yasmin and the other two carrying more fuel.

"Fine," agreed Anne. "It's fairly sheltered, too. I vote we use one of the blankets to make a kind of lean-to tent, and if we get our macs out of our cases we can use them as ground sheets."

"I know how to hang a pot over a fire," Gary volunteered. "We did it at Cubs' camp last year. Oh—have we got a pot?"

"No, but this can will do as well." Aban had been rummaging in her 'survival kit', the haversack packed with all kinds of necessities for just such an emergency as this. "See, I will empty out the powdered milk into this plastic bag."

"Good-oh." Gary went off to cut a stout forked stick which he stuck into the ground near the fire at an angle and soon a can of water was beginning to heat up over the crackling flames.

While small Jonathan and Heather were deputed to keep feeding the fire with handfuls of dry twigs, the rest of the party set about making a shelter, for the two elder girls at least were well aware of how quickly it would be dark and then the temperature, already low enough, would be dropping even lower with nightfall. Naturally, none of the travellers had any warm clothing with them. Aban and the three Northcott children had only thin cotton garments, coming as they had done direct from the plains. The Oake girls had lightweight anoraks, since it was often damp and misty at Leolali, and, fortunately, Mrs. Southgate had bought them both thin plastic macs in case they should need them immediately on arrival in England. Attracted by the gay colours, Anne had invested in one as well, so that at least they could hope to keep dry, but the lower temperature at this altitude was a greater problem. Already Aban was shivering in her thin sari, and little Heather's face looked pale and pinched with cold.

"You'd better wrap this around you straight away, Aban." Anne opened the emergency blanket bundle quickly. "Heather, you come and sit closer to the fire, and Gary, you and Jon can share this one with her. We'll use one to make the tent and that leaves the last for the girls to share with me. Gerda, you and Yasmin had better put on your anoraks and anything else you've got to keep you warm."

They all did as she suggested and while the three North-cotts huddled together the others swiftly made a tent-like erection overhead with the remaining blanket and tree branches. It was a flimsy structure but at least it shielded the party from the worst of the wind. Yasmin and Gerda piled chunks of rock and large stones to anchor the blanket edges safely, and with the fire blazing cheerfully the little camp seemed almost cosy. By the time Aban had handed round mugs of steaming hot coffee everyone was feeling warmer and better.

All too soon the daylight faded and the shadows of the mountains opposite rose higher until all the valley was plunged into darkness. Overhead, stars sparkled frostily but the moon had not yet risen above the peaks and beyond the comforting circle of firelight was a blackness that seemed almost solid. Little Heather, town bred and unused to the strange country, began to cry softly.

"I want to go home. I want my Mummy. I don't like it here," she sobbed, and at once Anne put comforting arms about her.

"Cheer up, Heather; we'll all be going home soon and in the meantime this is a real adventure you'll be able to tell all your friends about. Don't cry, pet. Here, cuddle close to me and you'll be cosy."

"I d-don't like the d-dark," the small girl wailed. "I'm frightened."

Anne's arms tightened reassuringly about her.

"There's nothing to be afraid of, Heather, honestly. We're all here with you, close to you. And, besides us, we know Jesus is here as well, only we can't see Him."

Comforted, Heather stopped crying gradually and by the time she had had a mug full of hot soup that Aban had prepared, together with a biscuit, she was cheerful again although rather sleepy.

Huddled under the blanket she shared with her sister, Gerda was unusually silent as they all sat about the fire sipping the hot soup.

46

"It's not very solid but it's jolly warming. I feel heaps better now," Yasmin remarked when she had drained her cup. "Don't you, Gerda?"

"Of course." The answer was curt, almost snappy, and in the darkness Yasmin's eyes widened in surprise. At that moment, however, the moon sailed into view above the mountains and the whole of the camp site was awash with clear cold light.

"That's better. Now we can see to get ourselves comfy for the night," Anne said briskly, and for a few minutes there was bustle and movement around the fire as everyone opened suitcases to take out whatever clothing they could, either to add to what they were wearing or for rolling up to make a pillow of sorts. Under cover of the general movement Yasmin nudged her sister.

"What's up, Gerda? Aren't you feeling well?"

"I'm all right. Don't fuss, Yas," the other girl muttered hastily and firmly before rolling herself into a compact bundle and settling down to sleep.

Not entirely reassured, nevertheless Yasmin had the sense not to press the matter further. The truth was, Gerda was making discoveries about herself and not liking what she found.

"I'm scared, just plain funky like that little kid Heather. I don't like all this dark around us or—or anything. I don't know if there are snakes or creepy-crawlies or animals of any kind around here and I'm scared white that there might be! I can't think how Yas and the others can be so calm—though I guess she's as scared as I am inside, anyway. Oh, how horrible it all is!"

Next moment she gave a smothered gasp of surprise as she heard Yasmin speaking.

"Anne, do you think—I mean, could we—wouldn't it

47

be a good idea if—if we all said a prayer together? It—it would seem right, somehow."

"I think it's an excellent idea," Anne said promptly. "In any case, it would be frightfully rude to God not to thank Him at least for having landed us here safely. 'Specially when you think what could have happened."

Accordingly, while Gerda lay rigid with a mixture of feelings, chiefly surprise, Anne led the rest in a thanksgiving, followed by the familiar Lord's Prayer and one for the night.

" 'Lighten our darkness, we beseech Thee, O Lord; and by Thy great mercy defend us from all perils and dangers of this night; for the love of Thy only Son, our Saviour Jesus Christ. Amen.' "

Then with cheerful 'goodnights' the whole party settled to sleep. Only Gerda was too disturbed to fall asleep at once. Somehow, it had never occurred to her that one would be rude to God by ignoring Him. Unexpectedly the realisation made Him seem much more real to her, more a Person than a mere Name in the Bible. In addition, her quiet sister's sudden outspokeness had thoroughly startled her. Yasmin rarely expressed opinions and ideas off her own bat, as it were. Usually she preferred to wait until Gerda had said almost all that was necessary and then agree or, less often, disagree.

To hear her quiet and backward-about-coming-forward sister speaking out so unexpectedly gave Gerda a rather unusual feeling, as if her world had turned upside down all at once.

It was not a peaceful night, nor a comfortable one. The ground was hard and unyielding and seemed to become steadily colder as the hours wore on. They had damped down the fire with tufts of coarse grass since the twigs they had gathered soon burned away and no one could stumble about in the dark to hunt for more fuel. Anne had kept a few handfuls of dry twigs beside her in readiness for the morning and meantime the fire smouldered slowly, giving out a little warmth and a thin column of acrid smoke. No sooner had everyone settled down to sleep than Heather roused them all with cries that an insect had walked across her face. By the time she had been pacified with lots of cuddling and a glucose sweet, Gary was complaining of a crick in his back, while Jonathan, Yasmin and Gerda were shivering with cold again. Aban used a few of the precious twigs to make the fire crackle cheerfully again and once more they all tried to sleep. No one was very successful. Apart from when they were making camp they had not been doing anything particularly active during the day, even Aban having had little work to do aboard the aircraft since it had only been scheduled to make a short flight. As a result, although they did manage to doze off for short periods of time no one was tired enough to sleep properly and to be able to forget the chilly discomfort.

The night was full of strange noises, faintly sinister, and all too often the moon seemed to sail behind the mountain peaks and cast long black shadows all down the valley. No one was sorry when the first pale fingers of dawn began to streak the dark sky.

"All the same," Yasmin thought as she lay huddled close to the others for warmth and watched the bands of light slowly widen over the peaks, "I reckon we're going to get fed up with this place even when it is daylight, because unless the people from that village arrive jolly early we shan't get to their place today. We may have to spend another night here. We'll have to do something to pass

49

the time otherwise it'll be awful." The thought at the back of her mind was that Gerda would find the waiting more trying than the rest of the party and when Gerda was impatient her temper suffered. There would be tantrums, and suddenly Yasmin was determined to do something to prevent them. At home in Leolali she had never bothered with prevention, simply putting up with events as they happened. Now, however, for reasons she had not yet worked out clearly, Yasmin felt differently about quite a number of things.

"Besides," she told herself rather muddledly, "it would be fearfully ungrateful to God if we started a row—and Gerda's quite likely to! After all, we could have crashed in that plane and instead we're here, alive and well."

Sherpas

7

"PORRIDGE? I DON'T KNOW IF I LIKE IT. I'VE never tasted it." Gerda looked at the steaming bowl rather dubiously. "We only ever had fruit for breakfast at home."

"You were much lower down, nearer to the plains, at Leolali," Anne pointed out. "In this cold atmosphere you need something hot and filling to start the day."

"Aren't these dried foods fab?" Yasmin said quickly. "We used to have powdered milk at home, of course, but I've never seen this porridgy-stuff before—and did you say there were *potatoes* in the survival pack, Aban?"

"Yes, indeed; in powder form. You just add water," the Indian smiled. "There, I think this is ready now, and we have sugar to sprinkle on the top."

The Northcott children looked curiously at the Oake girls.

"Haven't you really ever had any of this before?" Gary asked. "You must have lived out in the wilds."

"We did." Gerda was tasting the porridge cautiously. "Wow, it's hot! M'm. Scrummy! I like it." She accepted a second helping and then, the first edge being taken off her appetite, gazed around. "I wonder how soon those villagers will get here. I didn't see any houses when we were coming down to land. Did anyone else?"

"Oh no, we could not," Aban said quickly. "The village is over the ridge just beyond that very dark patch of trees. It is high up and the people will have to climb down to the river bed and then up again to reach us. I do not think they will be here until this morning."

Gerda's fine eyebrows drew together quickly in a frown.

"But you said it isn't safe to walk around at night. How will we reach the village in daylight if they are so late?"

"We won't," Anne joined in calmly. "The Sherpas—it's a Sherpa village—will stay here with us and then guide us back in daylight tomorrow."

"Then if we have to spend another night here I vote we try to build a kind of hut or something a bit cosier than this tent affair," Yasmin put in swiftly before her sister could comment. She could see disappointment and dismay in Gerda's face and knew that an irritable outburst would follow.

"Coo! Do you mean like a—a sort of native hut?" Gary chimed in, innocently helping out. "I could cut tree branches with my penknife—it's a super one and jolly sharp."

"That's a good idea, Yasmin," Anne said at once. "Yes, I should think that with all day to do it we should manage something fairly substantial. Finish your breakfast, all of you, and we'll start right away."

Gerda's lips parted to make a remark and then un-expectedly closed sharply and she said nothing. The younger girl was quite clever enough to see what her sister was trying to do, and that made her think. It also puzzled her again.

"I can see that Yas wants to stop me moaning about things," she thought. "It's all very well, but I don't like it here and—oh well, I suppose the others don't either, only they aren't grousing. H'm." Not very proud to realise that her juniors were standing up to discomfort and fear far better than she was, Gerda abandoned that line of thought and concentrated instead on the change she could see in her own sister. "I can't think what's got into Yas. She's so —different somehow. Not braver exactly but—*bolder*, more ready with ideas and answers and things."

With the full daylight the sunshine was soon warming the camping site comfortably although after the great heat of the Indian plains the air felt cool and fresh. Thankful to have something to do, everyone worked hard, scouring the ground for stones and gathering firewood while Gary, with Anne to help, sought out tree branches big enough to be useful in making a shelter yet not too thick to be cut with his knife. By the time Aban called them together for a midday meal of soup and potatoes, both made from the packets of dried food in the survival pack, a rough stone wall about a foot high had been built on three sides as a base for the new shelter. When they had eaten, the work went on again. This time they had to fix the long thin poles Gary had cut. These were put slantwise into the ground at one end, their tops crossing at what was to be the highest point of the shelter roof, and secured there to a ridge pole.

"Though how we're going to tie them without wire or even string beats me," Gary commented, rubbing his nose with a grubby hand.

This was a poser no one had thought of until that moment but they were not defeated for long.

"Belts," said Anne, followed rapidly by "Scarves" from Gerda, and "Creeper stems" from Yasmin. In the end, all three methods were used and if the result was not exactly the conventional shelter depicted in woodcraft books it was at least secure. Finally, the blanket was fastened as a lining inside the framework and then all that was needed to complete the shelter was to cover the outside with twigs and grass.

"And anyone who says this is an easy job ought to try it." grunted Gerda as she wrestled with a spiky branch. "It may be all right on a desert island where you've got palm leaves and stuff like that but it's not so good here. Even the grass isn't much use."

"It would be if we knew how to thatch properly—and if we had the string or twine as well," Anne pointed out, struggling to fix a spray of leaves firmly.

"Still, as long as we put some kind of layer on the outside it won't be too bad," Yasmin said hopefully, wedging a clump of mossy grass between two of the poles.

Gerda sat back on her heels and looked at her sister in exasperation.

"What's got into you, Yas? What's the big idea of all this 'jolly little ray of sunshine' act?" she demanded.

Unexpectedly Yasmin giggled.

"I didn't know I was that, exactly, but it isn't an act, anyway. I feel cheerful."

"You must be joking. Cheerful? In this place? Hasn't it occurred to you that even when—*if* we get to the Sherpa village it's going to be ages before we get anywhere else? We may be months before we're able to go to England."

"I realise that; I'm not daft," Yasmin retorted. She hesitated. All the old shrinking from arguments and the general wish to avoid trouble with Gerda was tugging her back from the new thoughts that were making her change her attitudes. Then all at once her rather muddled ideas became clear in her mind and she spoke with unusual firmness. "The thing is, I'm so jolly grateful just to *be* here, alive and well, after that plane business and I think the least we can do is to show it. Our gratitude, I mean. And —and well, I know we decided we aren't proper Christians at all but I'm going to try to be one from now on. After all, we found we needed God an awful lot when we were in the plane and I reckon it would be downright rotten to go back to ignoring Him like we used to do." She stopped mainly from lack of breath, having poured the explanation out at top speed through sheer nervousness. There was no doubt that the series of crises and upheavals the Oakes had suffered since Gerda's birthday had thoroughly jolted placid, easy-going Yasmin out of her rather negative way of life. In her terror during the hijacking, for perhaps the first time she had realised and experienced the nearness and reality of the heavenly Father so that quite suddenly Jesus Himself had become a Person to her instead of a Name in the Bible, however familiar. Once she had become sure of this central fact her whole attitude changed and she could even see dimly something of the reasons that led men and women like her parents and the Southgates to serve the Lord in uncomfortable places. Of course, at present her changed feelings were all rather vague and what she herself called 'fuzzy round the edges', but the main realisation of Christ's reality and Presence was clear enough.

Gerda was staring at her now, open-mouthed with astonishment. When had Yasmin ever made such a speech before or even declared herself so strongly about anything?

"Wow!" Was all Gerda could find to say at first before she recovered herself a little. Then she frowned over the tufts of coarse grass she was collecting. All at once she felt rather envious; Yasmin, the Southgates, her own parents, they were all so sure, so certain in their beliefs that they seemed to be armed against the fears and discomforts that beset everyone at times. In the girls' present situation Gerda knew quite well that both her sister and Anne and Aban were just as scared and uncomfortable as she was, but they were facing up to it in a far better way. Now, to quote herself, she was swithering, wanting and needing the reassurance of God's Presence in this lonely place and yet deliberately holding back from accepting Him because to do so must mean a change in herself. If she accepted and acknowledged Christ Gerda knew she must put Him at the centre of her life instead of herself, and that was the real stumbling block.

By mid-afternoon the shelter was almost complete and, as Anne remarked, if it was not exactly beautiful at least it seemed to be reasonably water tight and wind-proof.

"We'd better collect some more firewood while it's light," she decreed, "and then we'll have something to eat."

Tired as they were after their day of unusual work everyone saw the good sense of this and they scattered willingly, picking up every piece of dry wood they could find, however small. They had to search farther afield now since they had used so much material for the shelter. Energetic Gerda, accompanied by Gary, roamed far along the rough landing-strip in the search and was just preparing to plunge deep into the bush at the end when she heard voices.

Startled, the two children stood still, staring into the thick belt of trees and bushes. Next moment, several grinning, weather-beaten faces appeared among the branches and a few seconds later a party of men stepped out on to the open ground.

"Sherpas," said Gary. "I've seen them in pictures. Wonder if they know English?"

Gerda looked at the brown faces a little doubtfully for a moment but one man at least seemed to have understood Gary's remark. His grin grew wider and he nodded vigorously several times.

"Thak Kung Sherpa. Many climbs with Bara Sahib. Yes, English understood," he said clearly, and everyone else nodded and smiled broadly.

"Oh good! Have you come to guide us to your village? Will it take long? Come and meet the rest of us," Gerda said with relief.

"Yess," said Thak Kung comprehensively, although Gerda guessed that he had only understood a part of what she had said. The language barrier did not seem to matter, however, as with more smiles and cheerful chatter in their native tongue the Sherpas walked along the airstrip. As soon as they were in sight of the camp Gary yodelled loudly, an accomplishment of which he was very proud, and which brought Anne and Aban and the rest rushing out to see what was happening. The Sherpas looked at them with unconcealed amazement.

"No Bara Sahibs? No climbs?" Thak Kung asked; clearly a schoolroom and mostly female party was quite unexpected.

"Oh help, they thought we were an expedition," said Anne. "How do we explain a hi-jack?"

Fortunately Aban spoke fluent Nepali which most of the Sherpas seemed to understand, although imperfectly. Their wrinkled and weather-lined faces looked solemn as the situation was made clear to them and after a brisk discussion Thak Kung nodded gravely towards the little group of Europeans.

"Sherpas sorry, memsahibs. Make welcome to our village. You stay long time."

"I'm afraid that is very true," Aban said to Anne privately. "They have no means of communication with the outside world except at very long intervals. We are truly stranded here now."

Surprise for Gerda

8
The second night on the airstrip was a little warmer than the first but no more comfortable for Anne, Aban and their juniors. The shelter certainly kept out most of the cold wind; nevertheless there was nothing to relieve the extreme hardness of the ground and everyone was stiff and aching when daylight came again. In spite of this even Gerda greeted the day cheerfully for at least they had the prospect of leaving their isolation today. The Sherpas, who had spent the night huddled close about a roaring fire, were up and about as soon as it was light enough to see, laughing and joking and obviously unperturbed by the bleak surroundings.

Aban brewed up a quantity of hot coffee and after they had had this and a bowl of porridge liberally sugared the juniors were eager to set out for the village.

Finally they set off, the Sherpas carrying the luggage and Aban's survival kit, making nothing of the awkward loads. At first the way led steadily downwards from the farther end of the airstrip but gradually the narrow trail grew steeper and more broken so that the inexperienced Europeans were thankful they had nothing to carry, and Aban in her long sari and thin sandals nearly came to grief more than once. As they descended the sound of rushing water grew louder until its roar dominated all other noises as they reached the river itself.

"Yee-ow! Have we got to cross that?" asked Yasmin,

eyeing the tumbling grey waters uneasily. "Oh well, I suppose it *can* be done or the Sherpas wouldn't have come this way."

"Come on, girls. We have to cross higher up, according to Thak Kung," Anne called back to the sisters and with rather wobbly grins they followed the rest of the party upstream, along the river bank.

It was a nerve-racking walk over sliding and slippery stones entangled with moss and undergrowth, full of hidden potholes and snags to trip the unwary, with all the time the swiftly flowing water only a few inches below their feet. It was then that for the first time in her life Gerda discovered that she could be afraid of water in spite of her love of swimming. Before she had gone many yards along the track the menace of the rushing, swirling waters so close to her feet made her feel sick and giddy. Not that she had any notion of admitting the fact to anyone. She struggled on, feeling utterly sorry for herself until, unexpectedly, a hot sticky hand was thrust into hers and small Jonathan ranged up close beside her. His face was very white beneath its heavy sprinkling of freckles and as he met her look Gerda knew that the water was having the same effect on him as on herself. Yet, small as he was, he evidently did not intend to give way to his fear.

Gerda's heart warmed towards him and for the first time ever she was suddenly more concerned with a comparative stranger's discomfort than with her own.

"I don't suppose we've much farther to go like this, Jonny," she said with a fairly good attempt at jauntiness. "We'll hold each other tight so's not to slip, shall we? Do you reckon we'll be going up that mountain there or the one straight ahead?"

59

Chattering determinedly about anything that came into her mind she concentrated on taking Jon's attention away from the water as much as possible, and in doing so found her own sickness lessening.

It was hard and hot work to keep up with the Sherpas but Gerda had a very real fear of being left behind on that dangerous path so she hurried Jonny along energetically. They were all feeling the altitude now for although they had started out by going downwards from the airstrip to the river the whole valley was itself considerably higher than even the Oakes' comparatively hilly home at Leolali. Gerda was finding every movement an effort and only now did she realise that Anne and Aban as well as the three Northcotts must be feeling much more exhausted because they had spent most of their time in India down on the great plains.

"They must be feeling far worse than Yas and I do," she told herself, "and, if so, I'm jolly sorry for 'em. I will say, though, none of them's complaining."

Which was partly why she was grimly determined not to grumble herself. Gerda had her fair share of pride which had had to take a number of hard knocks recently. Nevertheless, it was not entirely pride that was making her plod on without complaint just now although she would have been puzzled to explain her feelings clearly.

If the trek along the river bank was hard, its difficulties paled into insignificance when the party reached the crossing point. Gerda and Jonathan came up to their leaders to find them grouped on a small triangle of flattish ground opposite a terrifying jumble of rocks and tree-trunks.

"This," said Anne with a casual air that certainly belied her real feelings, "is where we cross. The bridge gets washed away every monsoon so this is the best available for most of the year."

Jonny's hot little hand tightened on Gerda's and she did not need to look at him to know that he was terrified. She felt rather panic-stricken herself but at the same time it seemed important to her to help the younger child. Until now she had had very little contact with small children and in any case had always given them the same casual, uncaring treatment she bestowed on everyone outside her own family. For once, however, she could understand and genuinely sympathise with someone else who was as frightened of the situation as she was herself. Accordingly she made a great effort now and, swallowing hard, managed to speak with a fair assumption of calm cheerfulness.

"I expect it'll be O.K. then if Thak Kung and the rest help us across. Jonny's going to help me, anyway, because he's a boy. Those logs look firm enough and it isn't awfully wide just here. I suppose the Sherpas come this way all the time so it can't be too bad."

Before anyone had time for comment Thak Kung was organising the river crossing and they had to move on. With a Sherpa, sure-footed and grinning, on either side of them each of the travellers was carefully led across, from wet rock to wetter log, up and down, balancing precariously on the rock and wood that made such an uneven pathway amid the foaming grey water. Everyone was hot with fear and exertion and well splashed with spray but no one fell in or slipped too disastrously and in a surprisingly short time the entire party was safely standing on the opposite bank.

"D-did I help?" Jonny stammered a little, still clutching Gerda's hand and she gave him a breathless grin.

" 'Course you did, Jon old son. We held each other up, didn't we?" she assured him and he managed an uncertain smile as the terror faded. "Come on, we're a team, you and me. Let's show them how we can climb now."

"Good work, Gerda. Keep it up," Anne's quiet voice commented as Jonny moved forward obediently, following Yasmin and Heather up the start of a steep pathway and drawing Gerda after him.

No one had much breath left for chattering now as they all struggled slowly upwards with many pauses for the Europeans and Aban to rest. Nevertheless, in spite of the difficulty of the climbing and her increasing tiredness Gerda found herself feeling inwardly unusually peaceful and content.

"And that's a bit odd considering I'm aching in muscles I didn't know I possessed and my feet are ready to drop off, they're so sore and tired," she thought as she gave Jonny a boost up over a rough boulder and then scrambled up herself.

Now they were coming out of the narrow ravine-like valley and following a spectacular track up and along a great rock spur. As they climbed higher and higher they could see the sun shining on distant mountain peaks, making their snow crowns sparkle brilliantly against the clear blue sky. It was a wonderful sight but no one had the energy to appreciate it except perhaps the Sherpas and they were used to the tremendous scenery. Long before they had all climbed half way up the spur Thak Kung handed over his share of the luggage to one of the other men and with a grin swung small Heather up on to his back, while one of his brawny companions did the same for Jonathan. Somewhat to Gary's relief he was apparently judged man enough to walk unaided and so avoided the indignity of

62

being carried. Nevertheless by the time the party arrived at the summit even the most energetic of the girls was longing to sit down and rest. Instead, however, Thak Kung urged them forward along a last few yards beyond an out-jutting rock buttress and once there they had their reward. Ahead, the mountain swept back leaving a triangular plateau where stood the Sherpa village together with several small potato fields. A woman fetching water from a spring just outside the village soon noticed the travellers and set up a cry of welcome that brought people running from house and field. In a few moments it seemed that half the village was swarming out to meet them and led by Thak Kung the newcomers entered Lam-jura in the midst of a cheerful, excited, and exclaiming crowd.

With a fine sense of drama Thak Kung and the other men were evidently telling the rest of their people all about the hi-jacking amid a series of 'oos and ahs' of amazement before, as they came up to the first house, two kindly-faced motherly Sherpanis parted the excited crowd and ushered the tired travellers indoors.

"This is Thak Kung's own house," Aban managed to understand. "He is Headman, and these are his wife and his mother."

Five minutes later the weary party were all seated on thick brightly coloured rugs in a warm room, sheltered at last from the cold wind and already feeling rather drowsy as their kind hostesses bustled about preparing refresh-ments for them.

Heather and Jonathan did indeed fall asleep long before they had done more than sip their first bowls of hot fresh yak's milk. The other girls and Gary managed to keep awake but it was a real struggle to do so.

"Did you notice?" Yasmin murmured. "All the downstairs part of this house is a stable?"

"M'm. Good idea. Saves them going outside to feed the animals in winter," Gerda nodded sleepily. "Less trouble; I'm all for it."

"Well, for someone who doesn't like taking trouble over anything you did a pretty good job with Jonny today," Anne put in with a smile.

"I did?" Gerda tried to wake up properly but the warmth of the room and the softness of the rugs they were sitting on combined to defeat her after the cold and exertions of the journey. "He was scared," she muttered drowsily. "He's only little, too. It was the river, it rushed so, made us giddy and horrid."

"I know. So you thought you'd help Jonny, and you did. I doubt if he'd have been able to carry on without you."

Yasmin nodded agreement, shuddering at the memory.

"It was ghastly. I never thought I'd be so scared of a river," she said, and the memory roused Gerda a little.

"Nor me," she said with more emphasis than good grammar. "I was scared white I'd fall in. It made me feel all fuzzy and sick. And then Jonny's so tiny and he was being jolly plucky about things and I was so busy with him that I forgot the worst of it."

"It often happens like that when we're loving our neighbours in that way," Anne said softly.

The remark penetrated Gerda's drowsiness and she jerked upright in surprise.

"That's daft. I don't love Jonny," she said with her normal energy. "I only wanted to help him out of a sticky patch."

"I know, but don't you see, Gerda, wanting to help someone *is* loving," Anne said patiently. "The real kind of loving isn't all mushy sentiment and—and sloppiness; it's caring, like you did today for Jonny. Helping and wanting to make them happier and more comfortable. Now do you understand?"

Gerda stared at her for several seconds, trying to take it in through recurring waves of drowsiness. Finally she nodded slowly.

"Well, what do you know?" she murmured between yawns, "I've been a Good Samaritan and didn't know it. Hi-yah. Maybe this Christianity stuff isn't so impossible after all."

Lamjura

9

"WELL, WHAT EVER ELSE YOU CALL IT, IT WASN'T exactly a peaceful night but I was so tired it didn't seem to matter. Ouch! Am I stiff!" Anne stretched gingerly, wincing as strained muscles protested.

"It was lovely and warm, though." Gerda spoke drowsily still as she rubbed her eyes and tried to wake up. "Ooh, it's a bit smoky in here."

"Mrs. Thak Kung's getting the fire ready for cooking," Yasmin said. "Wow, I'm stiff, too. It was decent of them to put us up in here last night because I think it's their best room, but what do we do now, Anne? I mean, we won't be able to get away from here very quickly, I suppose, and we can't stay with the Kungs indefinitely. I'm sure they slept in with the animals last night, some of them, anyway."

"I'm sure they did, and you're right, Yasmin. We must try to help ourselves so that we aren't too much of a burden on the Sherpas while we are here. Thak Kung said he would send messengers down to—oh, I forget the name of the village. They have a radio there and a military post so they can relay the message to—to Katmandu, I think. It seems a round-about way but they probably know best. As long as our folk get the news that we are safe it doesn't matter how it comes. In the meantime, like you I think we can't stay here. It would be too much of a nuisance for the Kungs. Not that they'd ever say so but we're hopelessly overcrowding them. Aban, do you think we can hire a house in the village?"

Aban nodded in the semi-darkness of the room.

"I will see," she said. "It should be possible."

"What about cash? How do we pay them?" Gerda asked bluntly.

"We shall have to hope that they will trust us," Anne said after a dismayed pause. "I've only a few rupees with me. All the rest is in Travellers' cheques and I doubt if they'll be of much use here."

Before they could discuss the matter more, Mrs. Kung came into the room followed by two of her slender daughters, all three bearing large bowls that steamed and smelled savoury. The pleasant faced Sherpani and her children had not one word of English between them but with smiles and gestures they seemed perfectly able to make themselves understood. Mrs. Kung did know a little Nepali, however, and during breakfast Aban tried to explain the situation to her. It took a long time, with Mrs. Kung's limited grasp of the language, coupled with giggles and laughter from Neri and Sola, her daughters, and a chorus of smaller children who clustered in the doorway, bright-eyed and curious. Anne and the others watched their hostess's expressive face eagerly as it mirrored bewilderment and then distress and then, after a frantic spate of Nepali from Aban, reassurance and understanding.

As Mrs. Kung finally smiled and nodded and spoke to her children in a rapid flow of language, Aban explained, "She thought at first that we were despising her home, that it wasn't good enough for us to stay in. It would be an insult to her hospitality, you see, if we were not satisfied."

"Oh, help, did you manage to make her understand?" Anne asked quickly.

"Yes, yes, in the end. She says she will send Neri to ask Angma Dorje. He has another house since his parents died and perhaps he will let us use it. Thak Kung has gone to see about sending a messenger to Chalikumba—that's where the radio is for sending messages," she added and the gusty sighs of relief showed how anxious everyone had been about their isolation.

"It isn't that I mind being here," Gary explained defensively, "but our Mum and Dad must be worried stiff until they know we're O.K."

"I quite agree." Anne nodded. "The sooner our home folk know we are safe the better for them. Thank God for radio. A few years ago it would have taken months for a message to get through to the outside world."

"I just hope Dad isn't too worried about us," Yasmin murmured uneasily. "He—he isn't really well enough to have anything extra to bother about."

"I should think the doctors would have more sense than to tell him we're missing," Gerda put in with her usual vigour. "They wouldn't be so daft as to worry a sick man like that and I guess they won't let him see newspapers or listen to the radio news for a while, anyway."

"Gerda's right, Yasmin," Anne said quickly. "No one will be worrying your father with this affair. And by the time they think he's fit to be told it'll be O.K., because they'll be able to tell him we're found."

Reassured, Yasmin relaxed.

"So really it's a good thing Dad is ill, in a way, because he won't have to be worried," she said pensively. "It's Dr. and Mrs. Southgate and Gary's folk—oh, and Aban's family—who'll be worried sick. Well, I never thought

68

I'd be thankful for Dad's illness, but right now I am. Isn't it weird?"

"It is, but it does show how wrong we are to start blaming God the minute something happens that doesn't suit us," Anne pointed out just as Mrs. Thak Kung came back into the room all smiles and obviously full of news.

"She says Angma Dorje will rent us his house for as long as we must stay," Aban translated. "Come, we can go to see it now."

Nothing loth, they wriggled into anoraks and, in Aban's case, a thick jacket loaned by Mrs. Thak Kung before groping a way downstairs and so out into the clear, cold sunlight. A dignified young Sherpa awaited them in Thak Kung's doorway and after polite greetings they all walked along the stony track that was Lamjura's main, and only, street. The house that had belonged to Angma Dorje's parents was a small one, similar to Thak Kung's, but obviously it would be better for the seven stranded travellers to stay there than to overcrowd the kindly Sherpas.

"I don't suppose there are any furnishings, but we've got our blankets and Aban's survival kit so we'll manage," Anne said as they ceremoniously parted from their dignified landlord at the open door. "We'll be able to buy a few pots and pans for cooking, I expect, and anyway it'll be a lot better than camping out at this altitude."

Chattering cheerfully, they groped their way up the typical dark staircase to emerge into a clean, bare room with a balcony warmed and brightened by sunshine.

"This is fine," Anne was beginning when a stifled shriek came from below and suddenly Yasmin erupted into the room looking scared. She had been the last to enter the house, having stopped to take a stone from her sandal.

"Th—there's something m-moving down there," she stammered. "It's all black and horrid."

Startled, they all stared at her; then Anne rallied.

"Let me see. Where are the matches, Aban? Thanks." Lighting a twist of paper hurriedly fished out of her handbag she went to the head of the stairs, followed by Aban and the cluster of juniors.

The flickering light threw weird shadows over the rough walls below and lit up a pair of mild enquiring eyes set in a shaggy black face, Anne chuckled with relief.

"It's all right, Yasmin. It's a yak, quite a small one, too. Angma Dorje must be using the stable here as well as at his own place."

"Oh!" Yasmin looked rather sheepish and then joined willingly enough in the laugh against herself. "Daft of me, but I never thought of animals being here in an empty house."

"Well no, it isn't something we're used to at home, I admit," Anne allowed, quenching the torch quickly before it burnt her fingers. "Now, we'd better sort ourselves out and see what we need to make the place comfortable."

It did not take long for them to put their few possessions into the main room, which was unfurnished apart from two heavy wooden benches and a low table.

"Beds of some kind, or sleeping bags, are the first essential," Anne was just deciding aloud when the tramp of feet on the uncarpeted wooden stairs heralded visitors. Next moment Mrs. Thak Kung came into the room followed by three other smiling Sherpanis and several children. Everyone carried a bundle of some sort or a collection of pots and pans and bowls and in a very short time it was obvious that the kindly Sherpas knew exactly the needs of the strangers and were ready to provide for them. With much laughter and cheerful chatter among themselves it seemed that everyone in the village turned up during the next hour or so and by the time the last grinning small boy had disappeared down the stairs Angma Dorje's formerly empty house was fully furnished.

"Aren't they kind?"

Slightly dazed by all the commotion, the girls put the last of the bright hand-made wool rugs into place while Gary and Jonathan carefully stacked the small bundles of firewood so thoughtfully provided.

"Now we can make a fire and have a meal," Aban said. "Then we must go to fetch more water."

They ate their meal of potatoes and rather leathery meat at a low table set out on the balcony in bright sunlight. The air was crystal clear but with more than a hint of the ice and snow that could be seen on the tremendous peaks that towered all around, so that in spite of the sunshine it was only just pleasantly warm. From their lofty perch they could see a constant straggling procession of women and children going up and down the spidery stone tracks around the village, busy with their daily chores of fetching water and fuel, or tending the shaggy yaks who could be seen grazing on some of the slopes of coarse grass. Something of the sheer hardship of the Sherpas' existence impressed even the youngest children as they watched, and Gerda was particularly silent and thoughtful. When they had washed and dried the few dishes they had used, everyone collected a container of some sort and the whole party set off to walk to the spring. Aban led the way with Heather and Jonathan, holding their hands firmly so that they kept to a steady pace, for up at this height the air was thin and they were all suffering in varying degrees from the altitude. Gary followed, chattering to Yasmin.

Of the three Northcotts he seemed to have acclimatised quickly, as had both Yasmin and Gerda whose home at Leolali had been hilly enough to prepare them a little for the real mountains. Gerda dropped back now to walk with Anne who was clearly feeling the effects of altitude although she had said nothing in complaint. As Gerda herself was in a distinctly sober mood they struggled up the path in companionable silence.

"Ouff! Let's take a breather for a minute." Halfway up the steepest part of the track Anne sank down on to a flat boulder.

"Are you feeling all right?" Gerda asked rather anxiously and the elder girl shrugged slightly.

"Only a bit mouldy, thanks. I'll be fine in a day or two when I've acclimatised. Don't look so worried, Gerda. I'll be all right, honestly. Some people do take longer than others to get used to altitude, that's all."

Gerda's anxious face relaxed a little.

"Well, if you're sure," she said doubtfully.

"I am," Anne interrupted with some of her normal vigour. "Well, what now? Why are you looking at me like that?"

The rebellious junior heaved a gusty sigh, lowering her gaze quickly and scuffing a foot uneasily against some small pebbles on the path.

"I was just thinking how ghastly it would have been if you hadn't been with us, and if you got ill now it would be terrible," she said jerkily. "I mean, Aban's awfully nice, of course, but we don't know her much yet. We—I reckon we—we've got a terrific lot to—to thank God for, haven't we, really?"

"Thanks for the bouquet, but I'm sure you'd manage quite well without me if necessary," Anne spoke lightly enough but inwardly she was praying soberly for wisdom. She had realised from the first that with a complex character like Gerda it was very necessary to choose one's words carefully or with the best of intentions more harm than good would result. "As long as you don't try to do without God. I certainly agree that we all owe Him a tremendous debt of gratitude in this situation. I—hope we'll all remember it and not be ungrateful."

Gerda squared her shoulders and looked up, her face flushed.

"I have been," she said gruffly, "but I—I'm sorry. Will —will He let me start again, do you think?"

Gerda

10

"BUT DON'T YOU GO TO SCHOOL AT ALL?"

"No." There was a general shaking of heads, although everyone smiled or laughed at the same time. Then Torje, Thak Kung's eldest son, who like his father had a few words of English spoke for them all.

"No school here. Other villages—some—have school. Not us. Too poor."

"You don't know how well off you are," Gary said darkly. "No school, no prep, no lessons—super!"

"Oh, Gary, you don't really mean that," Yasmin said quickly as Torje looked puzzled, and Gary grinned sheepishly.

"No, p'raps not. It's a lovely thought though. Still school's not so bad even if it is a bit of a bind at times. Some lessons are fun, specially finding out about animals and things," he added firmly.

"I'm jolly sure I'd rather be going to school than sitting out in a field looking after a herd of yaks," Gerda said with conviction and the rest of the English party nodded agreement.

The travellers had been stranded in Lamjura for nearly ten days now and had made friends with all the Sherpa children as well as with their elders. In spite of the language barrier they all managed to make themselves understood with sign language and smiles and odd words picked up daily. It had not taken the juniors long to realise what

74

hard and frugal lives the Sherpas led and the contrast between their own comfortable way of living was being brought home to the Oakes and the Northcotts constantly.

Practically everything that they had taken for granted as part of their lives, the comfort of their homes, the plentiful and varied food they ate and the ease with which it appeared every day, was almost non-existent here in this Sherpa village. True, the houses were strongly built of stone and wood to withstand the bitter winter weather but they had few comforts by western standards. Every drop of water, for instance, had to be carried daily from the distant spring, every bit of fuel for cooking and heating gathered from the mountain sides, and food was only produced at the expense of continuous toil. Except in one or two of the wealthier houses, lighting was by small butter lamps, and since Sherpa houses do not have chimneys the living-rooms were either smoky or very cold. The richer villagers had perhaps a single oil lamp, brought by a trader from some Indian bazaar many many miles distant, and they managed to keep their rooms smoke-free by burning charcoal for cooking and heating, but even these refinements could not compare with western comforts that the English children had been used to all their lives.

Every Sherpa child was expected to work almost as hard as their parents, either in the potato fields or fetching water and fuel and caring for the herds of shaggy yaks which in Sherpa economy take the place of sheep and cows. The girls and women made clothes for the family, spinning and weaving and dying the yak hair, and yak milk and meat formed a large part of the usual diet, along with potatoes, tsampa (cooked barley meal), and yak curds, together with a small variety of vegetables. No one went to school in Lamjura, for there was none, and only one or two of the men, like Thak Kung, had ever been away from the village when they had sought work with climbing expeditions during a time of potato famine.

"And of course there's no doctor or nurse or hospital. They're much worse off than we were at Leolali," Yasmin said seriously and rather to her surprise Gerda nodded, equally serious.

"And how! We thought we were in the backwoods. Leolali counts as civilisation compared with Lamjura," the younger girl said. "What are we going to do about it, Yas?"

The question, totally unexpected and unusual coming from Gerda, startled her sister who could only gaze at her in silence for a moment. Before she could recover enough to answer Gary chipped in.

"How do you mean, *do* about it? What's there to do and, anyway, why should we? I mean, it's their way of life and nothing to do with us."

Gerda's normal self-assurance seemed to be less in evidence now and her oval face was rather red. Nevertheless, her small pointed chin rose in a determined gesture that her family knew well. Only, this time she was not demanding her own way, or indeed anything for herself.

"I mean, what are we going to do to try to improve things here for the Sherpas," she said earnestly. "After all, we're supposed to be Christians, aren't we, and to—er—love our neighbours enough to help them. If we don't try to do something we're like the—the folk who pass by on the other side when they see someone getting hurt."

"Coo! I suppose that's right." Gary was genuinely surprised and, with Heather and Jonny, suitably impressed so that they started arguing at once about what they could actually do for Thak Kung and the rest. Under cover of their chatter and the equally lively if incomprehensible talk of the Sherpa children, Yasmin edged closer to her sister to ask a question.

"Gerda, do you really mean that—about being Christians, I mean? I thought you said ..."

"I talked a lot of rot," Gerda said hurriedly, looking acutely embarrassed. "Don't rag me, Yas, please. I was a selfish idiot, I can see that now but, well, I've said I'm sorry and I'm trying to start again. Anne says I can if I'm truly sorry, and I *am*."

"Oh, good!" Yasmin breathed. "Honestly, Gerda, I'm jolly glad. I'm trying, too, and I am beginning to see a little of what Mum and Dad used to talk about. It—it isn't just Names in a Book—it's real."

Gerda nodded and turned in some relief to the three Northcotts who needed a referee for their arguments just then. Her change of heart was still new enough for her to feel shy about it and while the renewal of real faith in Yasmin had had the effect of making her a more positive person and more ready to speak her mind, having thought for herself, the reverse was the case with Gerda. Always more inclined to ask questions than her sister had ever been, she progressed towards the truth at a slower pace but her thinking was deeper. Once her sense of very real gratitude towards God had helped her to face up to her own selfishness Gerda had still been left with doubts.

"I do want to thank God and I will try not to be selfish," she had said privately to Anne one day when Yasmin and the three Northcotts had been having rides on some of Thak Kung's more docile young yaks, "but it's this idea of—of accepting Jesus as our Saviour that bogs me down.

I mean, I know He was betrayed and died horribly but what difference can that make to me now?"

"It's the difference between a vague hope and rock-bottom certainty," Anne pointed out, having done some intensive thinking herself during their progress to Lamjura. "Before Jesus came, God was simply the Creator, a wonderful but rather vague and terrifying figure about Whom men knew very little. Jesus, literally, brought light; He showed men that God is also our loving Father Who is ready to be patient and forgiving, and with Whom we live after death. Isn't that well worth knowing? And don't imagine you're the only person ever to have doubts, Gerda. What about Thomas, the disciple, who couldn't believe that Christ had risen until he proved it for himself? You know, the person who has always really clinched the matter for me was Simon Peter."

"How?" Gerda was sufficiently impressed to ask and Anne grinned slightly.

"Well, I suppose it's chiefly because I'm not one of those cool, calm and collected people who never flap in a crisis and I've never felt very brave about anything—even the dentist! But neither was Peter. By all accounts, he went into a complete flat spin when Jesus was arrested and was about as much use as a piece of damp chalk. He got so scared that he wouldn't even admit that he knew the Man Who'd been his close Friend for ages. That's how scared Peter was. But look what happened to him after Easter Day."

"He—he led all the other disciples and did healing and —oh yes, he stood up in public and told everyone about Jesus," Gerda said slowly, remembering the Bible study lessons she had endured so unwillingly.

"Exactly, and he was put in prison for refusing to be

silent and in the end was ready to give his life for the Lord. Don't you think that something pretty tremendous must have happened to cause such a complete change in a man? I've always thought it must have been his absolute certainty that Jesus was in fact all He claimed to be and that although Peter couldn't see Him any more he knew He was with him all the time, everywhere."

"I never looked at it like that." Gerda sounded startled and surprised.

"Well, you don't until you realise that the Bible stories in the New Testament are records of real living people and not just fiction," Anne commented and her junior gave a little wriggle of excitement.

"It's a bit—thrilling almost when you think of it," Gerda acknowledged with an unusually serious expression on her pretty face. "Thanks a lot, Anne. I think I'm beginning to see what it's all about now."

"You're very welcome." Anne smiled, with a tiny silent prayer of thanksgiving that she had been given the right words to say in dealing with the rebel of the Oake family. "If you take the trouble to read what Jesus Himself said about most things you'll understand even more."

"I might just do that," Gerda grinned unexpectedly. "I'll have a good chance as long as we're stuck here, anyway, because I do believe the only book in English in the place is the Bible. I've got the one Dad gave me years ago and Yas has a new one from her last birthday, I know."

"Gerda, Anne, come on, you two. Don't you want a ride?" Yasmin called just then and the conversation ended as they slithered down a rough track to the comparatively level grassy stretch of ground where the amateur yak-riders were trying their paces. Nevertheless, Gerda did not forget the talk. As soon as she was convinced of some-

79

thing she usually liked to act upon it, her energetic personality preferring deeds to words. Accordingly, quietly and unobtrusively, during the past few days she had been dipping into one or other of the four gospels and this time reading the familiar words with interest instead of boredom, and understanding much more in the process. One result was her feeling of concern for the Sherpas now.

"That's a good idea, Gary. We could teach them a little English while we're here, and send them books and things when we're gone. Then they'll be able to talk to any expeditions that come this way. We could start showing them how to read, too? What's that, Heather? Show the girls how to knit? Well, yes, we could if they don't already know." Gerda hastily intervened in the Northcotts' wordy battle.

"I'm going to show them how to play soccer," Jonathan said, scornfully rejecting knitting as being a particularly stupid feminine pastime. "It's jolly good exercise, better'n P.T."

"I know, let's give a party for them and have races and games like we do on Sports' Day," Yasmin suddenly suggested. "It would be something new for them, because they are always working so hard."

"Super. We'll do that. Let's go and ask Anne and Aban if they think it's O.K. and then Aban can explain to everyone." Gerda was all for dashing off at once but Yasmin stopped her.

"We can't this minute. They're seeing Mrs. Thak Kung about buying vegetables. And, anyway, hadn't we better plan a bit more first? We need a programme and we'll have to arrange a sort of party tea—and a few prizes for the games if we can manage it."

Gerda grinned and wrinkled her nose at her sister.

"Old sobersides Yas! You're right, of course," she admitted cheerfully. "O.K. We'll wait and have a family council on it this evening. Only, let's make it a really good 'do', a real celebration."

"What's there to celebrate?" Gary asked, rather surprised, but Gerda only laughed and changed the subject, although Yasmin guessed that for her sister there really was something special to be glad about now and to celebrate.

The Party

11

"WOULDN'T IT BE GORGEOUS JUST TO HAVE A nice hot bath with water that actually came out of real taps ..."

"... and oodles of soap and bath salts ..."

"... and big fluffy towels to dry on ..."

Small Heather Northcott started the conversation and even her brothers joined in, in spite of being as allergic as most small boys are to water associated with washing.

"We'll certainly appreciate water and bathrooms more after this experience," Anne put in her comment, "and lightweight buckets," she added with a grunt as she swung a heavy wooden Sherpa bucket away from the spring. "Don't fill yours too full, Heather, or you won't be able to lift it."

"I never realised before how much water we need every day," commented Yasmin, stepping back with her bucketful while Gerda took her place, moving carefully on the slippery stones beneath the water source.

In their life at Lamjura perhaps the biggest and most important chore of the day was the collection of water. Yet, as the elder girls at least realised, this was only one of the many tasks which would have been theirs had they been residents in the village rather than visitors. As it was, the Sherpas were quite ready to share their meagre provisions and crops with the strangers, trusting in repayment at some future date when the Europeans should manage to send money or food to them.

Anne and Aban between them were keeping a careful and accurate account of all that they had had to ask the Sherpas to supply and were very conscious that unless they were able to replace the food from outside sources before the winter came many of their friendly hosts would go hungry for a time.

"O.K. Is that the lot for now? Let's get back, then. I promised Neri and Sola I'd show them how to write the alphabet today." Yasmin lifted her bucket off the stony ground and started along the path back to the village.

"They pick it up jolly quickly, don't they? We're starting words today and Torje knows heaps already," Gerda said, following the rest downhill. "They're so frightfully keen to learn."

"They are, and that's half the battle won. I only wish I could learn Sherpa as quickly,' Anne said rather breathlessly for her bucket was large and heavy and she still had not completely acclimatised to the altitude.

"Still, you are trying to learn Nepali as well," Aban pointed out with a smile. She had lifted her bucket to one shoulder and was carrying it there with the peculiar grace of most Indian women.

"I suppose I am trying to run and walk at the same time," Anne acknowledged with a laugh. "Oh look, isn't that marvellous?"

They all stopped and looked where she pointed. The early morning sun had just cleared the two massive peaks that dominated the southern end of the valley and in doing so had drawn away the last of the mists that hung about the upper slopes. Now, in air that was suddenly crystal-clear again wave upon wave of snow crests and

83

ridges could be seen stretching away into the blue like a vast frozen sea.

"Super, but doesn't it make you feel small and—and sort of unimportant?" Gerda said slowly.

"I suppose that's not a bad thing for us to feel sometimes. I do like mountains, though," Yasmin decided. "They're heaps more interesting than very flat land."

"And a lot harder to walk on," grunted Gary whose sandalled feet were finding the uneven ground painfully rough. "If we're here much longer I shall have to wrap my feet round with rags like some of the Sherpas do."

The reminder of how ill-prepared they were for their stay at Lamjura sobered them all and they moved on down the path in silence. Then a tiny woeful sniff came from Heather.

"I don't *mind* being here," she said unsteadily, "but I would like to know when we're going home again."

"We'd all like to know that, Heather," Anne told her gently. "At least we do know that it won't be very long once the radio message gets sent."

"And if we keep busy the time will go much faster," Yasmin added encouragingly. "We do want to teach as many as possible of the Sherpas to read and write a little English before we go, and we've got to finish off the programme for the party—and that's only a week away now."

Gerda and Gary joined in quickly to discuss all the things they were interesting themselves in at Lamjura and the threatened homesickness was defeated once more.

Following their realisation that the Lamjura children had no chance at all of any education and Gerda's insistence that they ought to do something about it, the visitors were each teaching a small class of eager Sherpas as much English as possible every day. Thak Kung was reviving his own knowledge of the language as well and Anne had promised to raise the question of providing a school at Lamjura with the proper authorities as soon as their sojourn in this remote spot was over.

"We don't want to alter drastically or to ruin their way of life," she had explained, discussing it with the Oake girls, "but if they can all receive some education they'll be able to learn as well how to make even better use of their farmland, and perhaps one day have a Sherpa doctor and a nurse to help them when they're ill."

"It wouldn't be right to try to turn them into city people or to make them forget all the things they do for themselves, like weaving and—and things," Yasmin had said earnestly.

"No!" Gerda put in with her usual vigour. "It would be ghastly for them if they grew all soft and useless like some native people do when they start copying western ideas. I've heard Dad say often that it's the unkindest thing in the world to try to make people imitate a completely different way of life that isn't at all suitable to where they live. It's funny," she went on pensively, "I never bothered before to wonder what he meant but I know now all right. It would be awfully stupid and unkind to try to turn the Sherpas into city slickers."

"It would be quite wrong, too," Anne agreed. "They are a wonderful mountain people and we want to help them continue that way, only perhaps with a few more of the good things that we have, like education and medicine and hospitals."

"And perhaps when they can read English they'll read the Bible and find out about Jesus," Yasmin pointed out hopefully. "Because they don't seem to know about Him, do they?"

"No, and I reckon that would be one of the best things of all for them to learn," Gerda put in a little gruffly, because she was still self-conscious about her change of heart. Nevertheless, like Yasmin, she was every day becoming more aware of the value of accepting Jesus as one's Saviour, and the constant sense of His Presence with them in the harsh and alien world of Lamjura was a comfort that she would never have realised so quickly, much less acknowledged, elsewhere.

Now, the seven completed the journey back to the village in record time with the precious water, so busy were they in discussing all that they wanted to achieve before they finally left Lamjura. Naturally the three Northcotts were more interested in the forthcoming party than in the more serious work that the older four were trying to do, but even Heather and Jonny rather enjoyed the novelty of actually teaching other children and were quite proud of their pupils' prowess. Since there was no such thing as a schoolhouse nor a regular schooltime, the amateur lessons went on at all hours and in all places, the teachers going with their pupils to help in shepherding the yaks or gather fuel or potatoes as they taught.

With plenty to keep them occupied during the day, and often an invitation to join a particular Sherpa family for an evening meal followed by a cheerful singsong, the time passed fairly quickly so that when the day of the proposed 'English party' came Anne and the rest scarcely realised that this was the beginning of the third week since they had set off so happily from the Southgate home to fly to England.

To everyone's relief the day was a fine one, with only a gentle breeze to temper the sun's heat, and from early morning there was great activity in Lamjura. Officially the party was for the Sherpa children as a slight return for all the kindness and hospitality the unexpected visitors had received, but from the first it was plain that the entire village intended to join in the festivities.

"If we use the two tables pushed together and set them up in the courtyard we can put all the food on them," Anne suggested. "Then everyone can watch the fun while they're eating."

"A kind of buffet. That's a good scheme," Gerda agreed at once. "If we put everything indoors we'll all be smoke-dried and see nothing anyway."

"What do we do?" Gary wanted to know, encouraged by Heather and Jonathan.

"You could be in charge of the races," Yasmin said quickly. "You've got the list we all worked out, so now you can see that all the bits and pieces are ready—you know, the spoons and ties and things."

"Super. O.K. we'll get cracking." Very pleased to have been given so important a job to do the three juniors became happily busy for the rest of the morning.

"Are you sure we have enough prizes?" Yasmin asked as she helped to cover the tables with a colourful cloth.

"It'll depend on how many turn up but at least we have something for the winner of each race we've listed," Gerda said cautiously. "We've raked out every single thing we can spare anyway, so they'll have to be enough. We've only the clothes we're wearing left."

"I don't suppose prizes will be too important as long as everyone enjoys the party," Anne commented. "I just hope we've provided enough food. Still, Mrs. Thak Kung has promised we can dash over and borrow anything if we run out before the party's over."

"It's a queer kind of party tea." Yasmin surveyed the

87

plates of food critically as the three girls helped Aban bring them from the house.

"I've never made cakes from barley flour and yak butter before, that's certain," Anne retorted, "but they don't *look* too bad. I only hope our guests' digestions can cope with our cooking, that's all."

"As long as they all have plenty of tsampa and tea and potato crisps they'll be happy," Aban laughed. "Oh look, here are our first guests coming already."

With tiny shrieks of dismay the four scattered to tidy themselves and succeeded in being downstairs ready to greet the arrivals formally at the courtyard entrance. Clearly the villagers were regarding the occasion as an important one for in twos and threes and family groups they arrived at Angma Dorje's house with suitable dignity, in their best clothes, and with everyone carrying katas, the ceremonial scarves which it is Sherpa custom to present to guests and visitors on special occasions. Soon Anne and her companions were nicely enmeshed in flowing scarves as the courtyard filled with happy-faced, chattering Sherpas and their children. Finally, when Aban and Anne were sure that all the guests were present, discounting the uninvited ones, Gary rang a borrowed yak bell to attract attention and when comparative silence had fallen Aban made a little speech of welcome in her fluent Nepali which Thak Kung translated sentence by sentence for those who only understood the Sherpa language. Then, as Gerda remarked later, the fun really started. Under Gary's excited direction and with Aban and Thak Kung as interpreters the children were lined up in age and size-groups and a kind of sports programme started.

There were egg and spoon races, only the eggs were small potatoes and often balanced on pieces of wood where the supply of spoons had given out, and ordinary sprint races, an ingenious obstacle race over and under all the tree branches and stone heaps that could be arranged and, finally, a three-legged race. This last was a great novelty to the Lamjurans and gales of laughter went up as pairs of eager Sherpas struggled to the winning post.

Anne and her juniors had ransacked their luggage for tiny gifts to present as prizes, as had Aban, and there were beaming faces all round as the delighted winners received notebooks, picture postcards, pencils or ball point pens as their reward.

"Now we shall all eat and drink," Aban announced, when a cry went up and everyone turned to look towards the place where the mountain path leading to the village rounded the great outjutting spur. Two figures could be seen approaching and Aban quickly translated the Sherpas comments. "It is the messengers who went to Chalikumba for us—to send the radio message."

Return

12 "Oh, what are they saying? aban, can you understand? Did the message get through?"

Nearly dancing with impatience the juniors gathered about their interpreter, wishing that their own smattering of the Sherpa language were enough to help them to understand what was being said. Needless to say, the entire gathering, including the hosts and hostesses, had left the party at a run and hurried out of Lamjura to meet the returning messengers. Thak Kung had sent two of the sturdiest and most reliable of Lamjura's young men to make what was a fairly hazardous journey across country to the larger village of Chalikumba. They were travel-stained and tired now but still smiling cheerfully and full of graphic descriptions of their journey. Aban turned quickly to the excited juniors, smiling.

"It's been quite an adventure for these two," she explained. "They got to Chalikuma only after several mishaps—including a landslide—and, yes, the radio message has been sent. It was delayed, though, because something had gone wrong with the transmitter and the people at Chalikumba were waiting for a new spare part to arrive; that's why it has taken so long for them to return."

"But what's happening now? Are we going to be rescued?" Gerda wanted to know and even Anne looked eager for the answer.

"Yes, indeed. A special helicopter is going to come for us—one moment," Aban swung round to fire a rapid series of questions in Nepali to the messengers. "Ah yes, the authorities had to allow them at least five days to make the journey back here and have arranged to come to the airstrip for us three days afterwards. And that will be on the day after tomorrow for it has taken Parkay and Temba six days to come home."

"Wow! That only gives us tomorrow to clear up, because I suppose we'll have to get down to the airstrip good and early on the day," Yasmin said, rather startled. Somehow, now that she knew she was leaving Lamjura she felt quite sorry to part with the cheerful, generous Sherpas who had become such good friends during their enforced stay.

Obviously the others felt much the same and it was very clear that the Sherpas themselves were saddened at the prospect of seeing their young visitors leave so quickly. The lively party atmosphere faded as the news spread around the gathering and as they all started to escort the returned messengers into Lamjura the general attitude was sober and rather sad.

"This won't do," Anne said swiftly. "Today's a celebration and we mustn't spoil it for them. Aban, tell them that although we know we have to go so soon we shall never forget them or their kindness and we shall write to them often—and try to get them their school and hospital and everything else we can."

Aban nodded and ran on a little ahead before turning to face the villagers as they entered Lamjura. Scrambling up on to a heap of stones, ably assisted by Gerda and Gary who had run with her, she attracted everyone's attention and started to speak. Thak Kung, his pleasant face grave, stood beside the path ready to translate the Nepali into Sherpa as before. As soon as he heard Aban's first words the gravity left him and he was smiling as he translated to the villagers. They heard him attentively and then one by one the smiles and laughs came back so that by the time Aban's little speech came to an end they were all in a happy mood once more.

"Let's go on with the party," seemed to be the general idea and together with the foot-weary messengers they all crowded into the courtyard of Angma Dorje's house again. Somehow they all found seats on rugs and cushions or an odd bulk of timber, and Gerda, Yasmin and the North-cotts made haste to carry around the trays of thin wafery crisps of potatoes and bowls of tsampa and curds, while Anne and Aban dispensed tea at the table, having bor-rowed Mrs. Thak Kung's largest pots and pans for the occasion. The gentle Sherpani had also showed the elder girls how to make one or two delicacies beloved by the Sherpas, such as tukpa, noodles in a stew of meat and onions, and little strips of meat cooked with garlic. Every-one ate Anne's barley cakes with apparent relish and enjoyment in spite of the fact that to Western eyes they looked decidedly odd.

Finally, as the sun dropped behind the tremendous peaks that surrounded and enclosed the valley Gary and Jonathan built a big bonfire in the centre of the courtyard, with some help from their elders, and the company settled down to sing some rousing Sherpa songs. Called upon to entertain in their turn, the Northcotts obliged with a fairly accurate rendering of a seashanty, 'Shenadoah', followed by Yasmin and Gerda with a negro spiritual, 'Were you there?', and then Anne rounded off the proceedings with the great Cwm Rhonda tune for a favourite hymn

92

Guide me, O Thou great Redeemer
Pilgrim through this barren land

The elder girl's voice was not a strong one but it was rounded and golden with every note true and her audience showed how much they appreciated it by listening in breathless silence. They could not understand the words, of course, but obviously something of their beauty did touch them. At the end they all clapped loudly and Thak Kung said something to Aban who smiled and answered at some length. The Lamjura headman and all those near enough to hear and to understand nodded gravely.

"What do they say? Did they like it?" Yasmin asked eagerly.

Aban nodded.

"They wanted to know the story of the song and I told them it is about God and His great care for all of us. This thought is new to them, you understand, and they want to know more."

"Oh help, and we've so little time left," Yasmin said in dismay and Gerda was equally surprised to find herself suddenly wishing they were staying longer in Lamjura. No less was she amazed secretly to realise how eager she was to pass on the good news of Christ's Gospel to those who had not heard it.

"Well, what do you know? I'm beginning to feel like a sort of missionary, even if I can't do the preachy bits," she told herself. "Anyway, it's something I never dreamed of before. It's an odd sort of sensation, really, but now that I'm beginning to see what a super Person Jesus was and *is* now, I'm keen for everyone else to know about Him, too. No wonder Mum and Dad worked so hard at being missionaries, because they'd known Jesus for ages longer than I have. I do see why, now."

Equally eager with Gerda, Yasmin and Anne were already telling the bare outline of the greatest Life ever lived to the attentive Sherpas. Interpreted by Aban and Thak Kung it was a slow business but everyone enjoyed it and when at last the villagers began to go home they had much to talk about and obviously the party had been a great success in more ways than one.

"We've given them something to talk about and to discuss, anyway," Anne remarked as the tired girls helped Gary and Jonathan bring in the rugs from the courtyard. "We can leave them a couple of Bibles, so that when he's made some more progress with his English Thak Kung will be able to read the Gospels to them. We must try to get them the school, though."

"We must try," Aban answered seriously. "It will take some time but we must do it if possible."

"We'll do it," Yasmin said with sudden confidence. "After all, God wants everyone to know about Him and about Jesus so He's sure to help make it possible in the end, isn't He?"

"You could be right," Gerda agreed, stifling a yawn with some difficulty. "Wow, I'm whacked. It's been quite a day."

"Heather's nearly asleep," Gary said with brotherly scorn. "I say, we'll be able to help in the school business, won't we? I mean, our Dad's an engineer not a missionary but he'll want to help the Sherpas, I'm sure."

"The more the merrier," Anne assured him. "Yes, of course you'll be able to help, Gary; we'll *need* you. We must talk it over tomorrow. I think we've all done enough for today."

"And how!" Gerda murmured tiredly, and the rest

agreed as they prepared for bed as quickly as possible and soon there was silence in Angma Dorje's house, apart from the soft snufflings and movement of the yaks in the stable below.

The next day, their last in Lamjura, seemed to flash by. Admittedly, as Gerda remarked, there was very little packing of luggage to do as they had given all but their essential clothing and one or two other items to the Sherpas, but there was the house to clean and, with the help of Thak Kung's children, most of the furnishings and cooking utensils to be returned to the villagers who had lent them.

Mrs. Thak Kung had offered to see to the remaining few items after the visitors had gone. It was a lengthy business as it seemed as if nearly everyone in Lamjura wanted to call on them and say a personal goodbye so that almost before they realised it darkness was falling once again and they were eating their evening meal before going to bed in Angma Dorje's house for the last time.

Next morning, Anne and Aban were up as soon as the first grey wash of light was beginning to disperse the thick darkness. Lighting two small lamps, they dressed quickly and roused the juniors.

"It can't be time yet," mumbled Gerda, sleep still tugging at her eyelids.

"Yes, it is. Don't you want to go home?" Anne said bracingly and the younger girl sat up with a jerk, wide awake.

"Come on, Yas, it's THE DAY!" she said in clarion tones that effectively roused the rest of the sleepers. "Ooh, is that coffee I can smell?"

"Yes, a treat for our last breakfast here." Aban handed her a steaming mug. "Sherpa tea is very good ..."

"...but it's an acquired taste," laughed Anne, receiving her cup gratefully.

"Specially when they put rancid butter in it," grunted Yasmin. "I'm not complaining," she added quickly. "Everyone's been so absolutely super to us here and I'm jolly grateful to them all in spite of some of the queer things we've had to eat and drink."

"And so say all of us," agreed Gerda, draining the last of her drink. "That was good. It's jolly cold in the morning's still. Is there anything to eat?"

"Porridge coming up," Anne told her. "Wash and do your hair, all of you, and by the time you've finished breakfast will be ready. We don't want to be late starting, so buck up, everyone."

They hurried, washing in the ice-cold water brought from the spring the day before, and then getting into their warmest clothes before sitting down to bowls of hot porridge, carefully hoarded from Aban's survival kit. During their stay in Lamjura they had lived on Sherpa food as much as possible, but now that the end of their enforced holiday was in sight Aban was using some of the dwindling stock of European food. They did not linger over the meal but, even so, footsteps and voices were sounding from the courtyard before they had quite finished clearing up, so that the last few moments were something of a scramble. Then they were all hurrying down the dark stairs and out into the cold dawn air, where quite a party had assembled. They said goodbye to Mrs. Thak Kung and Neri and Sola and Torje with real regret and were brought near to tears when they saw how many of the villagers had risen early in the darkness to see them off.

"Goodbye, goodbye, we'll never forget you all. Thank you for everything."

96

"Sho, sho (hurry, hurry)," Mrs. Thak Kung smiled gently, although her eyes were sad, urging them to go for they must arrive on the airstrip in good time for the helicopter.

"Tuche che, tuche che," the juniors chorused, these being two of the first words of Sherpa they had learned and meaning 'thank you very much'.

Thak Kung raised an arm in salute and began to lead the way along the dark track, swinging a lantern to light the way. Anne and the rest followed after him, and half a dozen other Lamjurans, including the grave-faced Angma Dorje, each carrying a lantern completed the company. The trek back to the west had begun.

England at Last

13

"Ooh, I'm glad to be going—but I'm sorry, too." Yasmin sounded finely muddled about it but the others knew what she meant and laughed in sympathy. They were all in a mood that was a mixture of excitement, happiness, apprehension and sadness so that tears and smiles were very close.

"Goodbye, Thak Kung, and everyone. Sit tight, all of you, the pilot says it might be a little bumpy." Aban's English had become much more colloquial after spending nearly a month in close company with Anne and the juniors.

"I don't mind as long as it gets us to Mummy safely," Heather said.

Less than half an hour ago they had boarded this helicopter and now they were droning steadily along the valley with the tiny airstrip disappearing astern. The trek from Lamjura to the airstrip had been made in excellent time, for all seven of the hi-jack victims had done so much walking and hard scrambling during their enforced stay in the isolated mountain village that even small Heather made light of the rough journey down to the river and then the short sharp pull up the other side of the deep gorge to their original landing place. Admittedly, both Jonathan and Gerda looked askance at the tumbling grey river waters and the apology for a bridge once more but even their original fears were less now and they helped each other across the worst parts quite cheerfully. They had barely had time for a quick brew of tea at the site of their camp hut when the helicopter had appeared like a peculiar kind of bird flying along the valley and no sooner had it landed and everyone had been introduced to its smiling Nepali Army pilot and his navigator than they had to say goodbye to Thak Kung and their other escorts and climb aboard.

And now they were leaving the shadowed gorge and flying westwards over ridge after ridge of mountains.

It was far too noisy inside the helicopter for conversation to be easy and the seven passengers crouched on their rather uncomfortable seats, half dozing and dreaming as the aircraft droned on. Then at last the navigator turned round to smile at them and then point ahead.

"Kathmandu," he said, and effectively roused everyone again.

They crowded together to look down on the wide fertile valley that was such a contrast with the harsh terrain of Lamjura. Here the great mountain walls stood well back and the land was green and laid out in a mosaic of neat fields and pastures, with whitewashed houses looking like toys scattered on a carpet. Almost before they had had time to realise it they were coming in to land at the airport and arriving at the place famous for being the jumping off ground for most of the great mountaineering expeditions of the Himalayas and particularly for the ascents of Everest.

"Phew! What a scrum!" muttered Gerda.

Inevitably, as the returning victims of a hi-jacking that had made world news, the little party was met by the ubiquitous Pressmen and news-cameras as soon as they left the helicopter but fortunately both Dr. Southgate and Mr. Northcott were there with Embassy officials and after surprisingly few formalities and delay the little party found itself organised into two cars and driving towards Kathmandu city itself.

"Are you sure you're all right, son? And you, Heather, and Jonny?" Mr. Northcott clutched each of his three children in turn again and again as they drove past carefully tended paddy fields and then into the outskirts of the city where picturesque old houses leaned towards one another in the sunlight as if bowed with the weight of their years. Dr. Southgate, no less moved but more in command of his feelings, merely held Anne very close for a few moments at the airport and then greeted Yasmin and Gerda and Aban before asking questions.

At the guest house in the Embassy compound where they were to spend the night the luxury of hot baths and a European-style meal were the order of the day. Then, as Gerda remarked, clean and in their reasonably right minds the real talk began.

"Of course, it must have been much worse for you all at home because we knew we were O.K.," the once rebel junior said seriously at one point. "It must have been grim for you."

"You could call it that," Mr. Northcott agreed tersely.

"Are you sure no one has told Dad we were missing?" Yasmin wanted to be quite sure but Dr. Southgate was definite about it.

"Absolutely positive, Yasmin. You've no need to worry about that."

"He's really far too ill to be told anything much, isn't he?" Gerda looked straightly at the doctor. "Oh, you needn't worry about trying to soften things for us, Dr.

Southgate. I guess Yas and I have both—er—grown up a bit since we left Leolali. And—and we can take things far better now. You see, we know we'll always have help to bear them."

"Er—stiff upper lip and all that, eh?" Mr. Northcott said a little uneasily, and was totally astonished by his own small daughter.

"Oh *no*, Daddy. Gerda means that she knows Jesus is always here to help her—and us, too. Knowing about Him and trying to do what He wants is much more important than being brave, even."

"Well, what do you know?" The bluff engineer muttered and Dr. Southgate chuckled softly.

"'Out of the mouths of babes ...'" he quoted. "Quite right, Heather. And now I think you've all had enough excitement for one day, so to bed, everyone. You, too, Anne. We'll talk again tomorrow."

Scarcely able to realise that less than twenty hours ago they had been waking up in the cold darkness of Lamjura's dawn, the weary travellers were not sorry to do as they were told and soon all seven were sleeping peacefully. Next day, Anne and the Oake girls said goodbye to Aban who flew off to Delhi with the Northcotts.

Heather was rather tearful about the parting, in spite of longing to be with her mother again, and even Gary and Jonathan were suspiciously gruff as they shook hands manfully.

"Never mind, once we're all in England we'll be able to meet again, perhaps quite often," Yasmin said with determined cheerfulness.

"In any case, we'll be writing to you often about the Sherpas," Gerda added her quota eagerly and the threatened tears were averted.

"We won't forget you, either, Aban." Yasmin hugged the slim air-hostess affectionately. "We'll write, and perhaps one day you'll be on one of the European routes. You must let us know and we'll try to meet."

"Of course, and a message to the airline will always reach me," Aban assured them. "You know," she went on seriously, "we shall none of us ever be quite the same again after our stay in Lamjura. I think we have all learned much—and we shall not forget how good God has been to us."

"Aban's right there," Gerda remarked as she stood with Yasmin and the Southgates watching the plane disappear towards the south. "I thought we lived in the back of nowhere at Leolali but Lamjura showed me what a lot I had to be grateful for at home."

"And now—England. I can't believe we're really on our way at last," Yasmin said three days later.

This time the girls were aboard a jet plane high above the Mediterranean. They had flown from Kathmandu and had a joyous reunion with Mrs. Southgate and Anne's brothers before setting out once more on their interrupted journey to Europe. "All the same, now it's over I wouldn't have missed it for anything."

"You've got to be joking!" Gerda retorted, and her sister giggled suddenly.

"Not really. You see, I might never have met a real live yak," she said demurely.

After a moment's stunned silence, Anne and Gerda chuckled appreciatively.

Nevertheless, as the great aircraft flew across France and ever nearer to England the girls were serious enough. In spite of their newly found faith in God's goodness and in the loving Presence of the Saviour both Yasmin and

Gerda were feeling secretly rather apprehensive about the future. Quite apart from their father and his grave illness, they were facing the prospect of meeting their only other living relative, Aunt Elizabeth, a total stranger, as well as having to live an unfamiliar life among more strangers. Even Anne would not be with them after they landed in England, for she must travel straight on to Cambridge from the airport and the Oakes would be going in the opposite direction to Cornwall. Anne herself was very conscious that she must leave the juniors and, guessing something of their feelings, did what she could to help them.

"Remember, you two, that you'll be in England and you can telephone me any day. I've written my phone number as well as the college address on that paper for you, so if you want a natter you've only got to call me."

"Super! I hadn't thought of that." Gerda's rather gloomy expression cleared. "Sometimes you do want to speak to someone—it's sort of—a—closer feeling than writing," she added more earnestly than lucidly but the others understood what she meant and sympathised.

"Much better," Yasmin agreed. "We'll ring you when we've settled in and tell you what it's like."

"You do that," Anne said cordially. "Don't forget it's cheaper to phone in the evening so if cash gets scarce save your calls till then. You don't know how much pocket-money you'll get, remember."

Heartened by the assurance that they would at least have one friend to talk to if only by telephone, Yasmin and Gerda managed to say goodbye to Anne with a fair assumption of cheerfulness as they separated at the air-port. One of the airline staff had been deputed to see the two juniors safely into the correct train in London and so Anne was able to give up her charges with the certainty that they would be despatched on the last stage of their long journey without difficulty.

"What happens when we get to Cornwall we just don't know," Gerda said philosophically as they settled in their reserved seats and the train clattered with slowly increasing speed over the network of lines leading out of the great metropolis. "Still, at one time I thought we'd never get this far even."

There were very few passengers on the train and they had a compartment to themselves for most of the time. However, the guard had been asked to keep an eye on them and since he had daughters of his own he had a fatherly concern for them, coming in as often as his duties permitted to point out and name places of interest as the train carried them westward across southern England.

They reached Exeter in mid-afternoon where they had to leave the express and board the small two-coach train that wound its way slowly up to the moors where for the first time the girls began to feel the tangy, bracing air of the west country. After the noise and heat and vivid colours of India and the speed and clatter of London everything seemed quiet and placid and soft-toned here, and the creamy Devonshire burr of the local train's few passengers sounded strange after the high-pitched sing-song tones of the Indian voices the girls had known all around them since childhood. At last the small train slid to a halt in the high moorland town that was the end of the line. Once more Yasmin and Gerda picked up their few items of luggage and stepped down on to the platform, uncertain what to expect. Would Aunt Elizabeth have come to meet them? Would they recognise her, or she them, if she did? Before they had time to do more than take a few steps along the platform a cheerful voice spoke from behind them.

"You must be the Oake girls. Yasmin and Gerda, isn't it? You poor lambs, I expect you're half dead with all that travelling. Come on, we'll soon have you home now." They swung round to face the speaker, a pleasantly plump young woman with twinkling brown eyes and rich chestnut coloured hair. "I'm Mrs. Tremayne. Your aunt asked me to meet you."

"Oh—er—how do you do?" Yasmin remembered her manners abruptly and nudged Gerda whose slim brows had drawn together in a faint frown. Startled and tired, she blurted out the thought uppermost in both girls' minds.

"Why didn't she come herself? Is Aunt Elizabeth ill?"

Some of the twinkle went from Mrs. Tremayne's eyes as she answered reluctantly.

"No, Mrs. Hillyer isn't ill but I'm afraid—well, you see, she never goes out, anywhere."

Aunt Elizabeth

14

"I'M AWFULLY SORRY, I DIDN'T MEAN TO BE rude. It's really very kind of you to come to meet us," Gerda apologised promptly, blushing furiously.

"Not to worry." Mrs. Tremayne flashed her an understanding smile. "Come on, hop in. We've a fair drive before us." She led them to a large shabby estate car in the station yard, saw them and their luggage safely stowed and then took the driving seat herself. "The fact is, girls," she said quietly, swinging the car out on to the road, "your aunt has been something of a recluse ever since she came home to Ruanstowe after her husband died. To my knowledge she's not stepped outside the Manor Farm grounds once in the past five years."

"Not even to go to church?" asked Yasmin in astonishment.

"Especially not to go to church, I'm afraid." Mrs. Tremayne sighed sharply. "You must understand, girls, that she has had a very sad life and with some people they cannot forget or forgive the tragedies that come to them. Perhaps now that you have come to live with her, and particularly when Dr. Oake is at home again Mrs. Hillyer will feel differently. My husband is the minister at Ruanstowe and we would dearly love to see the Manor Farm pew occupied in church as it always used to be before old Mrs. Oake—your grandmother—died." She glanced at the girls' serious faces and went on quickly. "Now, you mustn't start thinking of your aunt as some sort of ogre or difficult person. Mrs. Hillyer is quite friendly and charming. It's just that she doesn't feel she can mix with people outside her own home."

"Oh well, after all, she hasn't had anyone to be company for her," Yasmin said optimistically. "Things will be different now."

" 'Course they will," Gerda agreed. "She'll have us to—er—encourage her and if she comes out with us it won't be like going alone, will it?"

"Very true." Mrs. Tremayne nodded. "Let's hope you are right." The car was out of the narrow streets of the little moorland town by this time and as she accelerated along a clear road the minister's wife changed the subject. "We went to see your father in Plymouth yesterday. My husband and I, that is."

"How was he?" Yasmin asked eagerly. "Shall we be able to see him soon?"

"Yes, you'll be able to visit him this week—I'll take you in on Friday. In any case, they may be transferring him to the hospital at Starford very soon and that's only five miles away from Ruanstowe. Then you'll be able to see him every day," Mrs. Tremayne assured them and then had to concentrate on her driving as the car threaded a slow way through Starford itself and its busy cattle market.

It was market day and although all the buying and selling were over by this time of day the little town was still full of cars and livestock and large cattle transporters. In spite of all the interest and bustle Gerda had not failed to note an important omission in Mrs. Tremayne's assurances and as soon as the car had passed the worst of the traffic she put a question in her usual brisk, blunt way.

"You didn't say just how Dad is, Mrs. Tremayne. Is he still terribly ill, please?" For all her briskness there was a tremor in her voice and the minister's wife was sensitive to it. Nevertheless, she had summed up the girls fairly shrewdly and guessed that both would prefer the truth rather than vague assurances.

"He is still quite ill but there has been progress in this last fortnight, Gerda. He isn't in the intensive care unit any more and he is definitely much stronger. And, do you know, I'm sure that when he sees you two again he'll really forge ahead towards recovery. He's missed you both very much."

"Like we've missed him, only we were rather in the thick of things so we haven't had a lot of time to be mopey," Gerda explained.

"Yes, of course, you've been having real adventures. You must tell me all about it. Incidentally, Dr. Oake was never told that you were missing, only that there was a delay in flying you from Leolali. Well, now, this is the last lap of the journey for today—that's Ruanstowe village straight ahead. Manor Farm lies over to the left."

The girls craned forward eagerly. This was what they had dreamed of for so long in the heat of Leolali. They just had time to see a small cluster of colour-washed houses set about a village green close to a grey stone church and lych gate, and then Mrs. Tremayne swung the car to the left into a short lane. For a few hundred yards they drove between high hedges and then the way was barred by a pair of tall wrought iron gates. An elderly gardener was slowly opening these and just inside a tall slender woman stood waiting on the gravelled drive. Mrs. Tremayne drove in slowly and then stopped the car.

"Here they are, Mrs. Hillyer, all safe and sound."

Yasmin and Gerda scrambled out and looked at their unknown relative doubtfully, both feeling shy and awkward. Then Yasmin saw that their tall aunt was smiling a little uncertainly herself and she guessed that Aunt Elizabeth was as nervous as her nieces.

"Aunt Elizabeth, we're so glad to be here," Yasmin made a great effort to overcome her normal diffidence and Gerda was quick to back her up.

"It's super—like coming home at last," she said with such genuine enthusiasm that Mrs. Hillyer's rather sad eyes lit with sympathetic amusement.

"It is your home," she said in a beautiful rich voice that told Yasmin at least that her aunt was a singer. "I hope you will be happy here. Thank you so much, Mrs. Tremayne. I'm very grateful ..."

"It was a pleasure. 'Bye for now, girls." After a few more remarks Mrs. Tremayne helped the girls to unload their small quantity of luggage and then with a final smile and wave she left. Picking up their suitcases, the two girls followed close behind their aunt and for the first time took a long look at Manor Farm, their father's birthplace and now their own home.

Once there had been a great Manor House at Ruanstowe but it had been burned to the ground during the Civil War and its owners exiled for their part in the conflict. The great mansion had not been rebuilt, for the exiled family had never returned to Cornwall and much later some of the original stones had been used to build a small less pretentious house, the present Manor Farm.

Long and low, it was L-shaped, with honeysuckle and wisteria making pink and purple splashes of colour as they climbed its stone walls to the grey slated roof. White window frames and a sea-blue front door gave the place a cheerful look, and in country fashion the door was open wide. Unexpectedly Gerda, the matter-of-fact felt decidedly choky as she entered the square hall that was full of the scent of flowers mingled with the subtle tang left by generations of polishing woodwork and burning log fires.

"It's—just beautiful," she said huskily and for the first time Aunt Elizabeth smiled fully.

"I think so. I'm glad you like it." She moved a hand caressingly over the smooth newel post at the foot of the wide shallow staircase. "It's all that's left of—oh, so much that was lovely," she added in a low tone almost to herself and her nieces exchanged meaning glances.

"There's no doubt about it, Aunt Elizabeth's really on the wrong track about things," Gerda summed it up at bedtime nearly a week later. "You can see she's got into the habit of caring much more for things like—like this house, and the gardens, and flowers than she does for real people. And that can't be right or good for her, can it?"

"I should think not." Yasmin curled up on her bed in the large pretty room they shared and spoke emphatically. "For instance, she's always interested when we talk about Lamjura and the mountains but she couldn't care less about the Sherpas. 'Course, it's all part of this business of blaming God because Uncle Jack and her baby got killed in that accident years ago."

"Dad might be able to talk her out of it but he won't be fit for ages yet," Gerda said pensively, brushing her hair slowly as she considered the problem. "We'll have to try to do what we can till then."

Yasmin went pink.

"We—we can pray about it, anyway," she pointed out and Gerda nodded seriously although she looked a little impatient.

"Sure thing, but I'm all for *doing* something as well," she said, restless as usual. "One good thing, Aunt Elizabeth doesn't stop us going out or going to church ourselves even if she won't come with us, yet. I'm jolly sure she will one day, though. The only snag is it'll take time and I like action now."

"Me too, but I don't know what we can do exactly. We'll just have to keep on praying and see what happens."

Life was very pleasant at Manor Farm, especially after their spartan experience at Lamjura. It was many years since Dr. Oake's parents had actually farmed the land but most of the outlying fields were leased to active farmers so that some grew crops and others were pastures for sleek black and white cattle. The land close to the house itself was a thriving flower and vegetable garden, there were two greenhouses, and in the small orchard a few brown hens strutted and pecked happily. After the dust and heat of Leolali Yasmin and Gerda were fascinated and delighted with their new surroundings. It was, as they had said, a childhood dream come true.

Nevertheless, whereas a few months ago Yasmin would have drifted gently and dreamily through each day while Gerda enjoyed herself more energetically but equally thoughtlessly, both girls had changed considerably since Leolali days. Aunt Elizabeth did all the work of house and garden herself with the assistance of a 'daily help' who came on two mornings in the week and the elderly gardener, Endor, who pottered gently about each afternoon. Clearly Mrs. Hillyer expected to cope with the increased chores of an enlarged household as well but her nieces soon showed that they had no intention of letting her do so.

"Of course we'll do our share," Gerda said firmly on

their first full day at Manor Farm. "We'd better get into a routine now because when Dad comes home he'll need looking after and by then we'll be going to school and won't have so much spare time."

"That's right, so we'd better get used to our jobs now so that we'll be able to fit them in with school and prep. and stuff," Yasmin added her quota with equal determination.

Unused to dealing with young people, Aunt Elizabeth agreed rather limply.

"I must say I had no idea you would be so fond of housework and weeding and all the other chores," she commented after a few days had shown the girls to be regular and uncomplaining in the work they could do about the house and garden.

"We're not fond of them," Gerda said, cheerfully grubbing down deeply into damp soil to pull up the last inch of a dandelion root. "They're ghastly bores, most of them, but they've got to be done."

"It isn't fair for you to have to do them all for us," Yasmin pointed out, triumphantly waving aloft the lengthy weed she had just dug out. "Phew, he's a whacker!" She grinned rather shyly at her grave faced aunt. "It's all a part of—of loving your neighbour, isn't it? Caring enough to help, whatever the job."

"I—see." Mrs. Hillyer looked at the two eager faces steadily for a few moments and then went on with her part of the work in a very thoughtful silence.

Cry from the Shore

15

"IT'S SUPER! DAD COMES HOME NEXT WEEK and Aunt Elizabeth's getting more—more knowable." Thus Gerda in a cheerful mood.

"That's not good English—I'm not even sure that it *is* English," her sister retorted. "What do you mean, *knowable*, if there is such a word?"

"Don't be stuffy, Yas. You know what I mean. When we first came she was like a—a statue, not hard exactly but as if she kept herself inside a shell. You couldn't get to her or see how she felt or—or if she felt anything at all. A bit like a solid ghost, if you see what I mean."

"You and your descriptions," grinned Yasmin. "Oh, I see what you mean, all right. I suppose it's like Mrs. Tremayne says, Aunt Elizabeth seemed to die inside when her husband and baby were killed. She's awfully nice, of course, but you never know if she feels anything, do you?"

"No, but I'm sure she's beginning to," Gerda said optimistically. "Anne thinks so, too. I told her last night how surprised Aunt Elizabeth was when we started doing our own chores every day. She says if we can only go on showing her—Aunt E., that is—that we care she'll come round gradually."

"Good. It's super being able to have a natter with Anne. Did she tell you she'd had another letter from Aban?"

Chattering steadily about the Southgates and Northcotts and, inevitably, their Sherpa friends the girls ambled slowly across the short thymey grass that covered the clifftops hereabouts. They had gone by bus in to Starford for their daily visit to Dr. Oake, now in the pleasant little cottage hospital there, and now they were walking back to Ruanstowe by way of the cliffs. It was a long walk but they were not in any hurry and made nothing of the miles. As they went they were busy discussing in particular how they could raise money to send schoolbooks and especially Bibles to Lamjura. To provide the school itself was beyond their means, but they knew that the Southgates were in touch with a number of people, Christian societies and business houses who were concerned with education in isolated areas, and from these it was hoped that the actual schoolbuilding and a teacher could be provided. The girls hoped to work out a way of giving less costly but equally important items, such as books and stationary, towards the project.

"When we get to school ourselves it'll be easier because we'll be able to get lots of other girls interested."

"Sure to," Yasmin agreed. "We have roped in the Sunday School here already and they're quite keen."

"Yippee!" Gerda gave a skip of enjoyment and stretched her arms widely, looking around appreciatively at the green clifftops with their dappling of grazing sheep, the red and brown and grey cliff faces slanting steeply down to a tumbled blue-grey sea, for it was high tide, and the cloud-flecked blue sky.

"All this," she said in answer to Yasmin's questioning look, "all sort of fresh and free and just what I've always wanted. It seems too good to be true. And even the bits I don't like, like Dad being more or less an invalid now, well, it's all a lot easier to put up with. You know, Yas," she went on, unusually serious, "when I think back to the awful rot *I* was nattering about on my birthday I—well, I just don't seem to be the same person. That's why I'm so dead keen on helping Aunt Elizabeth to get back to Jesus. She *must* or she'll never really live. We've proved it, haven't we?"

"I suppose we have." Yasmin's thoughts did not always go quite so deep as her younger sister's did these days but there was no doubt in her mind that for her, as for Gerda, life had really begun to have meaning and purpose and direction from the moment she had realised and admitted her need of Jesus as Saviour and Friend. With Him at the centre of everything the rest fell into place and even the inevitable upsets and unhappy experiences became bearable. Although neither girl was very demonstrative by nature nor given to expressing her deepest feelings aloud both knew with secret happiness that the change in them had given such real joy to their father that he had gained strength rapidly ever since they had come to Cornwall. Dr. Oake's health had been too deeply undermined for him ever to be able to work again the gruelling hours that had been his daily habit for so many years, and the girls knew that at best he would be a semi-invalid for the rest of his earthly life. The knowledge had hurt them all and yet had drawn the three closer together than they had ever been before.

"Never mind, Dad. You'll have to be the brains and we'll be the—the hands for what you want done now," Gerda had declared and the mere fact that his girls were taking their new situation so well was immeasurably comforting to their father.

"That's right, and you'll be able to write up all those notes you've made over the years on malnutrition and—

oh, I can't remember the medical words, but all the things you discovered at Leolali," Yasmin had added. "Gerda and I can learn to type them and perhaps they'll make a book one day," she added earnestly.

She was thinking of this now as they drew level with the headland that was in a direct line with Manor Farm and from which a narrow track led inland to the house itself.

"Dr. Southgate told Anne that with all Dad's first-hand experience he should be able to write a textbook that would be a standard work on his subjects," Yasmin remarked with satisfaction. "It's bucked Dad up no end and I really think he's looking forward to starting work on it as soon as he gets home."

"I expect he likes to know he can still do a jolly useful job medically even if he can only sit and write," Gerda agreed. She giggled suddenly. "All I can say is that he'd better give us a good dictionary if he wants us to spell those ghastly medical words because I'm none too bright on ordinary ones!"

"And how!" agreed her sister. "My own spelling's a bit wild. I think—listen, was that someone calling?"

"Don't be daft, who could be? There's not a soul in sight."

"No, but I heard—oh well, I expect it's the gulls. They make a din, don't they?"

Certainly the only sounds now along the cliffs were the screaming and mewing of sea-birds, the occasional bleat of the grazing sheep, and always the hissing and rumbling of the waves against the rocks. So far as the girls could see, they were the only human beings there and after a short pause to look around they ambled on towards the track leading home.

"M-Mummy! I want Mummy! Mummy!"

Sharply cutting into a brief lull in the gulls' screaming the thin wail came faintly and the sisters stopped abruptly.

"It is someone," Yasmin breathed, "but where?"

"Shush!" Gerda said sharply, listening. Then, as the cry did not come again she cupped her hands about her mouth and called clearly, "Where are you? Keep calling."

Almost at once the reply came.

"I'm here. Mummy, I want Mummy. I'm frightened."

"Over there." Yasmin pointed vaguely towards the cliff edge. Gerda nodded and moved forward, calling again, "Keep calling, we're coming, where are you?"

It was difficult to pinpoint the thin weak voice amid all the other cries and as they drew nearer to the cliff edge naturally the noise of the sea began to dominate and drown lesser sounds.

"It's someone caught by the tide, for sure," Gerda opined swiftly. "A young kiddie by the sound of it. Come on, Yas. If we lie down we can look over and see better."

Quickly but cautiously they crawled to the edge of the cliffs and then lying flat, looked down the steep face. The waves were lapping to within a yard or so of the base, throwing up fountains of spray where they hit the outlying tumble of fallen rocks, and at first the girls could not see the caller. Then Gerda spotted a blue-grey patch that was a deeper colour than the rest.

"Down there—blue anorak. Looks like it's wedged in the rocks. Quick, Yas, we can climb down over there—there are heaps of ledges and handholds."

"We'll have to look nippy, that water's coming in fast." Like her sister Yasmin was suddenly very white-faced as she saw the dangers but neither hesitated for more than a brief second or so.

Biting her lower lip in concentration Gerda lowered herself cautiously over the edge and began to creep downwards. The cliffs on this part of Cornwall's north coast were steep but seared and scarred with ridges and ledges that gave precarious foot- and hand-holds, slanting as they did at acute angles. At the back of Gerda's mind was the thought that climbing up again was likely to be far more difficult but she ignored that for the moment. It was problem enough to get down at present.

They made steady progress and in a surprisingly short time Gerda found she could jump down the last couple of feet to the beach. At once a swirl of water washed over her shoes and then receded. Clearly, they had not much time to spare. Floundering on the uneven, shifting jumble of pebbles and broken rock, the younger girl led the way to where she had seen the blue anorak.

"Over here, Yas," she panted, clambering round an enormous boulder and sliding down into a narrow gap between it and another even larger rock.

"Please help—p - please," wailed a small voice, and Gerda gasped aloud.

"Quickly, Yas. It's O.K., kid, we're here now." She crouched down to touch the wearer of the blue anorak reassuringly. He was a small boy, younger even than Jonathan Northcott, and the pale face he turned towards the girls was grubby and streaked with tears.

"It's my leg, it's jammed in, I can't get up," he sobbed, jerking aside in renewed terror as a swirl of water foamed menacingly into the narrow place between the rocks. In spite of the child's instinctive movement, however, only his head and shoulders remained untouched by the sea.

"Don't cry, old son," Gerda said with more confidence than she felt. "Here, Yas, help me to hold him more upright. That's it. Got him? Right, can you support him while I investigate just where he's wedged in?"

"Yes, he's not heavy. Don't cry, pet, we won't leave you," Yasmin comforted the child. "Are we going to be able to shift the rock, Gerda?"

"Shouldn't think so," her sister grunted, having tried. "But, look, he's wedged sideways. If we can slide him upwards until he's straighter we may be able to pull him out."

"Good idea. Put your arms round my neck—what's your name? Alan? Well, you hold me tight, Alan." Yasmin lifted him slowly, not without some difficulty in the confined space, for Alan was rather heavier than he looked. "Ouch!"

A larger wave than the previous ones broke sharply against the rocks sending cascades of cold water pouring down, soaking the girls and Alan thoroughly.

"Yow!" Gerda shook her wet hair out of her eyes, frowning. "If the gap's wide enough for him to fall into it *must* be wide enough for him to slide out," she muttered, inwardly sending up a desperate prayer for help because it was obviously not going to be possible to move those rocks and the tide was rising rapidly.

"I suppose his weight would have forced him in." Yasmin frowned over the problem, easing Alan's position slightly in her arms. "There must be a way—Gerda, see if you can get your hands in and take his shoe off. That'll make it easier."

"Yas, you're a genius!" Gerda acted at once, crouching low in the water and sliding her hands cautiously into the rock gap. Her groping fingers found Alan's foot encased in a stout leather shoe. She fumbled determinedly with the laces and loosened them before managing to tug at the shoe itself. It was immovable.

"Alan, wriggle your foot out of the shoe. Go on, you can, I've untied it," she urged and in sudden hope the small boy obeyed. There was a brief desperate struggle and then slowly but triumphantly Yasmin pulled him away from the rock trap, shoeless and soaked but uninjured.

After the Rescue

16

"It's no use, Yas, we aren't going to get any further like this. The kid's half asleep and we're whacked." Gerda squatted on a narrow ledge, breathing heavily. "We're above the tide-mark now, so it's safe enough here."

Yasmin nodded, too breathless to answer for a moment. It had been an exhausting struggle to get this far up the cliff face, encumbered as they were wih Alan who was too weary after his long ordeal to help himself much. Only the greater fear of the rising sea had kept him moving at all as the two girls had alternately coaxed and bullied him upwards and now, with his head in Yasmin's lap, he had collapsed, half dozing, on the slanting ledge that was the first place safe from the tide. Tired as she was, however, Yasmin could see several things very clearly and after a pause she spoke with unusual firmness.

"We can't stay here till low tide. Aunt Elizabeth would be frantic—and anyway we'd fall off in the end because it slopes horribly," she said. "Gerda, as soon as you've got your breath back you've got to go on alone. The coast-guards' place is on the other side of the next cove, nearer than home. They'll have ropes and rescue stuff. I'll wait here with Alan."

It was the only sensible thing to do and they both knew it. Nevertheless, Gerda looked doubtful.

"It'll be a ghastly long wait for you, Yas," she said in low tones. "Are you sure? I could stay . . ."

". . . no, you climb better than I do and you're heaps faster at running. Go on, Gerda. Only, don't slip and break anything yourself or we will be in the soup," she added with a quiver, half laugh, half sob.

Gerda nodded.

"I'll be very careful. You—you won't get dizzy and fall off the ledge, promise?"

"Promise. Buck up, Gerda, and—take care."

"And you. I'll be as quick as I can. Keep praying," she added with a brief glance of understanding that said so much more than the mere words. Both girls were thoroughly frightened of the situation, Gerda mainly of the swirling water below the climb she must make and Yasmin terrified of falling off the narrow slippery ledge. In spite of their genuine fear, however, both were just now experiencing a kind of inner calm, a feeling of being supported by an unseen yet almost tangible force, the certainty that Jesus their Saviour was truly close beside them.

It was this conviction that led Gerda to start up the cliff face once more calmly and steadily, while Yasmin put her arms more firmly around small Alan and sat tight against the rocks. From where she was on the ledge she could only watch her sister's progress for part of the way but she kept up a flow of cheerful comment that helped to reassure Alan and at the same time took Gerda's mind off the pounding, creaming surf below.

"I've made it! Yas, it's O.K., I'm up. Hang on, I won't be long." At last the triumphant call came floating down from the cliff top, thin, husky, and decidedly breathless.

"Super. Get cracking, Gerda," Yasmin called back and

then fell silent, steeling herself for the long uncomfortable wait.

Above her, the younger girl forced her tired legs to run towards the distant coastguard station. Help was closer at hand than she knew. Gerda had only just slipped and slithered down one of the several dips in the ground between her and the next headland and was struggling up the other side when two burly figures appeared on the crest of the next ridge.

"Oh, thank God, thank God!" Clutching her side where a cruel stitch was catching at her, Gerda waved and called with almost the last of her strength and as an answering shout came sank down on to the grass.

The hour that followed was almost dreamlike to the exhausted junior. Somehow she knew she managed to gasp out where Yasmin and Alan were, and then everything was taken out of her control. She was carried carefully back to the spot where she had struggled up and then set down to rest while the coastguards went about the rescue with calm efficiency. Police and other people seemed to arrive as if from nowhere, someone was using a walkie-talkie set, and then Yasmin and the little boy they had rescued were safely beside her on the cliff top for a few moments before all three were lifted and carried to Manor Farm.

"Oh dear, oh dear!" Aunt Elizabeth met the little procession at the door, startled and worried.

"We're all right, Auntie, honestly." Yasmin was quick to reassure her. "Just a bit tired and jolly damp, that's all."

Mrs. Hillyer rallied with unexpected swiftness, although her face had paled with shock.

"Hot baths then, and I'll make some tea," she said but

her gaze went past her nieces to Alan, grubby, wet, and tearful in the arms of a policeman. "Oh, let me have him. It's all right, pet, you're safe now." Cuddling Alan closely to her, she smiled at the girls over his towsled head. "You use the bathroom, girls, and I'll see to this little man in the kitchen. Mr. Brady, perhaps you'll come with me and tell me the whole story while I'm busy—oh, and Mr. Kivell, perhaps you'd come as well and make the tea for everyone."

The policeman and one of the coastguards were only too pleased to agree with her suggestion and, as Gerda said later, Aunt Elizabeth soon had everyone organised. Bit by bit the whole story was told, exclaimed over and told again, while pots of tea were made and emptied and the two heroines and their rescue victim alternately chattered and drowsed.

"Now this young Alan, he's not a local boy. Never seen him before in the village," Constable Brady said, "and it's too early for many summer visitors yet. I'll have to make enquiries. Likely he's been reported missing by now."

"I'll keep him here tonight," Aunt Elizabeth said quickly. "Oh, please, I'd like to—unless his parents are found quickly, that is. They must be so terribly worried about him."

"Of course. He'll be best here with you until they're traced. I'll be in touch as soon as there's any news, Mrs. Hillyer."

The policemen left and with them the coastguards, while Aunt Elizabeth put the drowsy boy to bed in one of Manor Farm's guestrooms. Then she returned to the sitting-room where her nieces were trying to keep awake.

"Now, girls, bed for you as well. You must be stiff and tired. I'll bring you something to eat when you're settled." She looked at them keenly as they rose obediently and, unexpectedly, put an arm around each slim waist. "I'm very proud of my brave nieces—and so will your father be when he hears of this," she said softly.

Yasmin's pale, tired face flushed with pleasure.

"Oh, do you think so? We couldn't leave anyone to drown, could we, specially a little kid."

"We were mostly scared white, anyway," Gerda put in honestly. "Only, well, knowing Jesus was with us helped so much. I—sort of—felt Him there all the time, didn't you, Yas?"

"Yes, I really did—like when we were in the airplane." Yasmin looked up at her aunt's suddenly stony face. "Isn't it queer, Aunt Elizabeth? We used to say we couldn't see anything in religion and all that but I suppose it was when ghastly things started happening, like Dad getting ill and then the hi-jack, well, then we realised that it really does work."

Mrs. Hillyer released the pair abruptly.

"It doesn't always; not when those nearest and dearest are taken from you," she said curtly.

Gerda stood her ground.

"B-but although it's sad and horrid, isn't it best for them?" she asked, greatly daring. "I mean, they're going Home to be happy with Jesus for ever. Shouldn't we try to be glad for them, even if it makes us lonely?"

Aunt Elizabeth drew in her breath sharply and for a moment Yasmin and Gerda both thought they had said too much.

"We—we don't mean to be preachy, Aunt Elizabeth," Yasmin put in nervously. "It's just that—well, we've more or less proved most things about Jesus for ourselves now and—and it does make such a difference from just being told about Him."

Aunt Elizabeth looked at the two earnest faces and slowly seemed to relax.

"Go to bed, girls," she said quietly. "I'll bring you a tray. No, it's all right, I'm not cross. You—you've given me something to think about."

Unexpectedly Yasmin gave her tall aunt a sudden swift hug and then with a grinning Gerda at her side the girls limped from the room.

They were sitting up in bed later demolishing a light but satisfying meal of chicken salad, cherries and custard, when the front doorbell rang and excited voices sounded in the hall.

"Alan's folk turned up, I reckon." Gerda cleared the last of her custard and sat back with a satisfied air. "Ouch! My back and legs hurt like mad but I feel heaps better now. I say, do you think Aunt E. thought we were fearfully cheeky to say what we did?"

"I hope not." Yasmin stifled a gigantic yawn with difficulty. "O-oh, I'm tired."

"So'm I but not really sleepy," Gerda admitted. Nevertheless within a very few minutes she was as sound asleep as Yasmin and neither knew any more until the morning. "Did Alan's folk come last night, Aunt Elizabeth?" she asked as the pair ate their usual hearty breakfast, none the worse for the previous day's adventure apart from stiffness and a few painful bruises.

"They did and they are upstairs now in the big guest-room," Mrs. Hillyer smiled. "Alan was fast asleep when they came and it was so late that I asked them to stay the night."

"Where do they live? They aren't locals, are they?" Yasmin wanted to know.

Aunt Elizabeth frowned slightly.

"It's quite disgraceful. They haven't any real home at all, just a ramshackle motor-caravan. That's how that poor child was able to wander away into danger. They had parked in a field at the back of the village. Mr. Rose, Alan's father, had gone to look for work and Mrs. Rose was over at Tilson's farm fetching milk."

"It must be grim, not having a proper home," remarked Gerda. " 'Member the hut we had to make before the Sherpas rescued us, Yas?"

"Do I! Wasn't it draughty? It was better than nothing but that's all. And if the Sherpas hadn't rallied round old Angma Dorje's house wouldn't have been much better."

"Perhaps we could help out with the Roses," Gerda said eagerly. "We could buzz around Ruanstowe and perhaps over to Starford and see if there's a cottage or something to let..."

"Super! We could start by asking old Bloss at the Post Office. He always knows everything local..."

"I—I have a small cottage that's vacant." Aunt Elizabeth spoke abruptly and flushed slightly as her nieces looked at her. "It—it's one that came to me as part of my legacy when our parents died. I don't know what condition it's in but it has three rooms as well as a kitchen and bathroom, I remember."

"Do you mean you'd let the Roses have it? How smashing! Let's go and see it right away." Gerda nearly overturned her coffee cup in her enthusiasm.

"It's on the other side of the churchyard," Mrs. Hillyer said slowly, and the girls remembered that she never left the Manor grounds.

Yasmin put a hand on her aunt's arm.

"Please take us to see it, Aunt Elizabeth," she pleaded. "It would be such a super thing for the Roses."

There was a pause and then Aunt Elizabeth seemed to make a great effort to speak naturally.

"I - I'll take you there when you're ready," she said, and abandoning caution both girls nearly smothered her in a gigantic double hug.

*   *   *

"So you see, Anne, it's all coming out in a super way," Gerda gabbled on the telephone a week later. "Aunt E. actually goes out now, and she's let Alan's folk have the cottage and given Mr. Rose a job helping old Endor in the garden because he's really past hard work now. And," she paused impressively, "guess what? She came to church with Yas and me yesterday. Isn't that terrific?"

"Splendid. Jolly good work, you two. Incidentally, I heard from Dad this morning. The pilot and all the other men in our hi-jack have just crawled out of the jungle to safety. They came down soon after they dropped us off and it's taken them all this time to get out. They're in pretty bad shape but they'll live, Dad says."

"I'm glad," Gerda said seriously. "You know, I'll always be grateful to them. They—did something for me."

"Me, too." Yasmin took her turn. "Just think, we're really able to help Dad more now, and Aunt E.'s happy again and the Roses have a home and the Sherpas will be getting a school eventually—and it all might never have happened if those hi-jackers hadn't made me meet a yak!"

"I wonder if the yak's recovered from meeting you," chuckled Gerda, and so had the last word as usual.